RECKON

Reckon

LOGAN PHILLIPS

THE UNIVERSITY OF
ARIZONA PRESS
TUCSON

The University of Arizona Press
www.uapress.arizona.edu

We respectfully acknowledge the University of Arizona is on the land and territories of Indigenous peoples. Today, Arizona is home to twenty-two federally recognized tribes, with Tucson being home to the O'odham and the Yaqui. The university strives to build sustainable relationships with sovereign Native Nations and Indigenous communities through education offerings, partnerships, and community service.

ISBN-13: 978-0-8165-5582-6 (paperback)
ISBN-13: 978-0-8165-5583-3 (ebook)

Cover design by Leigh McDonald
Cover art and interior design by Logan Phillips

Library of Congress Control Number: 2025030003

Printed in the United States of America
♾ This paper meets the requirements of ANSI/NISO Z39.48-1992 (Permanence of Paper).

R

CONTENTS

CONTENTS

RECKON

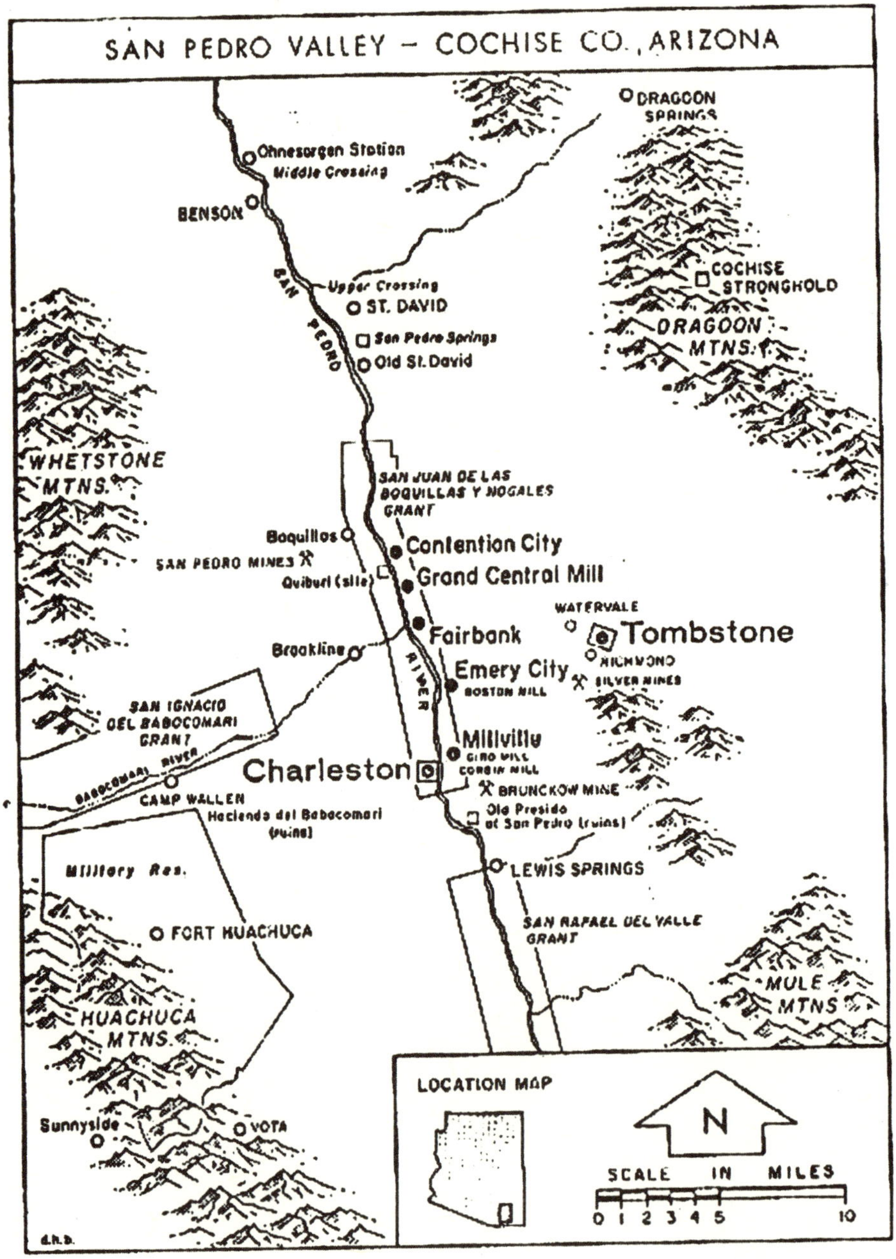
SAN PEDRO VALLEY – COCHISE CO., ARIZONA
DRAGOON SPRINGS
Ohnesorgen Station
Middle Crossing
BENSON
SAN PEDRO
Upper Crossing
ST. DAVID
San Pedro Springs
Old St. David
COCHISE STRONGHOLD
DRAGOON MTNS.
WHETSTONE MTNS.
SAN JUAN DE LAS BOQUILLAS Y NOGALES GRANT
Boquillas
SAN PEDRO MINES
Quiburi (site)
Contention City
Grand Central Mill
WATERVALE
Fairbank
Tombstone
Brookline
RIVER
Emery City
BOSTON MILL
RICHMOND
SILVER MINES
SAN IGNACIO DEL BABOCOMARI GRANT
BABOCOMARI RIVER
Millville
GIRO MILL
CORBIN MILL
Charleston
BRUNCKOW MINE
CAMP WALLEN
Hacienda del Babocomari (ruins)
Old Presido of San Pedro (ruins)
Military Res.
LEWIS SPRINGS
FORT HUACHUCA
SAN RAFAEL DEL VALLE GRANT
MULE MTNS
HUACHUCA MTNS.
Sunnyside
VOTA
LOCATION MAP
N
SCALE IN MILES
0 1 2 3 4 5 10

what we can all agree on
we call   history

&so   there is no   history

only broken adobe
&GUNFIGHTS

Tombstone Epitaph.

BIRTHS

LOGAN TIMOTHY PHILLIPS BORN APRIL 7

Tim and Judy Phillips' first child, Logan Timothy, was born on April 7 at Sierra Vista Community Hospital.

Logan Timothy, delivered by Caesarean section, weighed seven pounds, nine and one-fourth ounces. The new baby came home on April 13, Mr. Phillips said, and both he and Judy are doing fine.

Grandparents Bill and Mary Phillips, and Ron and Evelyn Eastin, live in Phoenix.

I was Toddlerme   learning to walk
in cowboy boots   over the wooden sidewalks

past emporiums of scorpions   trapped in glass :
paperweights   bolo ties   &lollipops

snake leather threaded in   ampersand   rattler print
&sand script   dustdevil belt buckle
postcards hats   sixshooters&**CAPS**

Toddlerme points the gun
at the man with the camera

— who shoots first ?

I didn't grow up there, you know. Don't call me *from* there.

Youngparents sold the **MUDHOUSE** when I was two. Cashed out before the bust — the **WOODHOUSE** burned down later. They built a new place in the southern sun, soaked in the western shadow of the Huachucas at **SUNSET**.

I grew up a boy looking at **TOMBSTONE** too. But I could see the actual hills from the secret holy spots where I'd spend my afternoons in the mesquite-marked grasslands. And when visiting the tourist trap of **ALLEN STREET** we'd first slowly cruise **OLD CHARLESTON ROAD** so Youngparents could see how the remaining house was getting on. If an agave they planted had flowered yet or if it was still biding its time. It's part of the reenactment:

YOUNGFATHER: To plant anything, I had to get through a layer of caliche about this thick.

OLDDAD: It's funny how it's all relative. When we moved over here, I thought this was the best earth I'd ever seen.

YOUNGFATHER and **OLDDAD** as **CHORUS:**
But a **BIRD-OF-PARADISE** would just grow wild over there.

To be clear, both characters are played by the same actor. Decades apart. The family dialogue is filled with refrains, bromides, myths. They change so slowly year to year that every so often I have to come by to check on them.

I place my hands back on the cement impressions of Kidme's hands from **'85**. They don't fit now, the cement dry as caliche.

Now folks keep an eye out. Coming up on the left, you can see my prize-winning poem from the Huachuca Mountain Elementary School Poetry Contest **'92**. Just so the score is settled, I'll say I would've won the whole district if it hadn't been for another kid's smarmy baseball poem. Mine was a fine piece about camping in the Dragoons, a rendering of wandering lights moving through the stacked boulders — stars, cars, or most likely something else entirely.

I've been writing the same poem since third grade. I've always had trouble saying exactly what I see. I should tell you up front : I'm also unsure what to believe.

But **WELCOME** *!* to the amusement park, the book filled with fathers, the tourist attraction of my manias. Maybe they're common, but in the town I'm *not* from, we talk it all up real big.

CHORUS: The town too dumb to die *!*
The town too crooked to croak *!*

Tombstone

ITION

TOMBSTONE, ARIZONA

City Accepts $30,000 Minimum For Graveyard

YOU want to know what was it like, being born in a town where so many died? To learn to walk where in **1884** a mob seized John Heath from jail, yanked a noose around his neck, and lynched him on the crossbar of a telegraph pole?

Tiny bootprints, stride askance. Dust kicked into sunbeam. Troubled then slowing, floating cursive curls.

Well, what I want to know is why **1983** looks like the olden days from here. Like **1883**. How the newsprint yellowed so, even though Youngmother treasured it to closet.

I'm not that old, the old man says. *I just come from a town that chose not to age. It's only been* 102 Years In The own Too Tough To Die { *sic* }

My *own* too tough to die? Acacia bramble, alkali crumble, chloride flats. Skinned knees, rose thorns. Cow shit and red ants the size of a trigger finger past the last knuckle.

This isn't poetry : this is the news. Everybody's dying of it.

The Epitaph's big news? There's **New operators of BOOTHILL. City Accepts $30,000 Minimum for Graveyard.** Including 3 percent of gross sales from the gift shop.

That's not gross, it's what any city does. Profit from the labor of the dead, then pretend it doesn't.

102 Years In The
own Too Tough
To Die

ol. CIII. No. 26

In Tombstone we're just wiser. We profit from the *dying* of the dead too. **Yesterday's Discards, May Be Today's Cash.** That's what industry there is in a ghost town.

The Business of Being What You Were. **Restoration work on Schieffelin Hall at an estimated cost of $24,000.** Repair the adobe, paint the cracks back on. Rip up the pavement on **ALLEN**, hide the power lines. It's what employment there is: haunt the visitors, spook the bills right out of their wallets. Go to work, get shot with blanks, be rushed to Sierra Vista Community Hospital.

Folks will pay good money to get this close to the dead. Put a fence around **BOOTHILL**, a ticket booth to make the rent. Mostly **OBITUARY** & so little **BIRTH**.

You really want to know? Pay me **20¢** to read all about it.

Yesterday's Discards, May Be Today's Cash

Only I can tell it. I'm qualified. Kiddad wore boots before I did. And true to life, I'm the one **BORN IN TOMBSTONE**.

Just because I hate **GUNFIGHTS** doesn't mean I never learned to quickdraw. Damned if I don't pretend cowboy better than the best pretend cowboys.

I'll tell you. Let you in on the secret they won't tell you in Tombstone :

there's an older graveyard underneath the Dollar Tree. But here's the biggest secret of all :

it was like being born anywhere. Keep your **20¢**. You don't need to buy a ticket.

You're already standing on death.

Don't believe me? On the way out of town, stop at the old Circle K, the one that was torn down. Buy a map, the one with a stagecoach on the front. Unfold it.

Let's see . . . shortest route from Fort Huachuca to Indian Wells. How far exactly to Starvation Canyon? To Skeleton Canyon? From Oury St. past Bloody Basin Road through Apache Pass, down Allen St. to Fremont, past Clum's *Epitaph*. See?

The **MAP** is an **OBITUARY**. Every point a tombstone, a monument to graveyard operators. Follow me, I'll show you.

RANDOM SHOTS

From The Epitaph's Twelve Bore

The Devere family has always figured prominently in Tombstone history so it is only fitting that Boothill Graveyard stays "in the family." The Deveres probably know as much local lore as just about anyone else in town.

Keeping the graveyard open 365 days a year could become thorny at times. But nobody promised the new operators a rose garden at Boothill.

DID YOU KNOW ?

--the Chamber of Commerce used to be a hospital.

--that eight rattle snakes were loose in the Casino Saloon when the volunteer Fire Department fought the fire in 1979.

--the second floor of what is now the Arizona Territorial Museum was used to hold dances.

--there used to be another bar in the basement of Pete's Bar called "The Sump" and it was owned by Shorty Madrid.

Tombstone Tailings

Flowers OK After Fumbled Fake Fall

During one of the Vigilantes shootout skits on Allen Street, Sunday, April 10, Wes Flowers took a fatal (blank) shot and a planned fall against a stage prop but lost his balance and hit his head on the pavement, Vigilante member Vic Mooso said.

Despite his experience in faking fatal gun wounds and executing convincing falls, Mr. Flowers "fell pretty hard" on the pavement, Mr. Mooso said.

Mr. Flowers was taken by ambulance to Sierra Vista Hospital Monday morning when complications from the injury apparently developed. His condition was monitored for three days at the hospital before his release on Thursday, April 14.

Mr. Flowers, security chief for Tombstone Exploration Inc., was once the national champion fast-draw artist. Mr. Flowers is still recognized as one of the best in the United States, Mr. Mooso said.

"It's all part of the game," said Vigilante member **Jim Ellsberry** of the unfortunate accident, adding, "We've all gotten banged up out there."

Fewer falls

Stuntman switch to songwriter a change of note

By EDWIN S. FINKELSTEIN
Citizen Staff Writer

From Old Tucson stuntman to composer and folk singer seems like quite an about-face. But Steve Eastin has made the switch as easily as he used to fall off roofs.

At 24, Eastin has just finished a movie Eastin has just ished a movie about rodeoing and cut a record of both the background music for the film and a number of his own compositions.

The flavor of the songs comes, he says, from his small-town background in Colorado. Eastin's voice is different. It's somewhat gravelly and has charm and quality — a cross between Mel Torme and a male Teresa Brewer — if you can imagine such a thing.

It's the right voice for the songs he sings.

"The film, called 'Twister, is a story about a boy growing up to ride competitively," Eastin said.

Courthouse Intruder Sets Off Alarm, Goes Batty

An intruder in the old county courthouse led Tombstone police on a wild chase the night of July 18, as he whizzed down the hallway and circled the mining room shrieking hysterically.

Three squad cars answered the alarm at 10 p.m. and a rash of policemen quickly searched the building. They found no one except a frightened bat.

National Park Service Ranger Tim Phillips said the courthouse often has bats in its belfry.

"They get inside through the cupola and set off the alarm three to four times each summer."

However, park officials are not positive how they enter the building or where they come from.

"They're mysterious bats," Mr. Phillips said.

A board has been placed between the belfry and second floor in hopes of preventing further intrusions.

On April 1, an independent television company out of New York will come to town to shoot 15 one-minute scenes around town, including a shootout at the O.K. Corral. They will bring a satellite dish with them which will beam the scenes live to Europe.

Law and Disord

April 11 — Dan McMurtrie arrested for assaulting a wom Big Nose Kate's.

Other reports that po responded to included: tresspass, four thefts, two pu assists, three false alarms, one r for ambulance, one accident as two reports of criminal damage, report of vandalism, two poss prowlers and a fight. The police responded to two arson-suspe fires and two reports of bad che

Saturday, May 29— Barb Kingsolver of Tucson was fined speeding.

The wooden gate that faces A Street at the O.K. Corral gave Eccleston Jr. several splinters i finger as he adjusted a locking that had been jarred loose Satur June 12.

Gleeson Is Ric

Renewed Interest I Town's Mining District

By STEVEN GRAUBART
Epitaph Staff

Gleeson is called a ghost tow some, a paradise by others.

At the turn of the century, Gle was a thriving mining and ranc town of 5,000 people. Today, on people live there. Snowbirds the number at the trailer park time to time, said Danny C tiansen, longtime resident of ghost town.

Mr. Christiansen owns the C tiansen Ranch just north of t His family has lived in Gleeson the 1800s.

"My grandfather, Hans C tiansen, was one of the first se in the San Pedro River area. He claim to 15 million acres of land. can see his claim in Book Tw Tombstone's Miscellaneous D and Records. Wyatt Earp's mi claims are in that book too," Christiansen said.

WEATHER

April continues to blow hot and cold. It may be too early to put away winter woolens but on some days short sleeves and cottons are beginning to feel right. The rain has given us a shower of wildflowers, with Mexican poppies ablaze along area highways. The National Weather Service forecasts a dry, mild Saturday with some clouds and increasing wind on Sunday. It will be windy and cooler throughout the state on Monday.

There was 0.10 of an inch of rain on April 7 and .04 of an inch on April 8, bringing the total precipitation for the year to 6.37 inches.

	High	Low
April 6	53	32
April 7	46	34
April 8	56	33
April 9	67	36
April 10	77	44
April 11	62	48
April 12	51	40
April 13	54	32
April 14	62	34
April 15	78	39
April 16	81	50
April 17	81	53
April 18	73	53
April 19	78	46
April 20	64	53

l. CIII, No. 26

The cowboy participants in the O. K. Corral fight ate breakfast here at the Chandler Milk Ranch the morning before the shoot-

I CONFESS I DON'T GIVE A GOOD GODDAMN WHERE THE COWBOYS ATE BREAKFAST

DOES that make me a bad historian? I guess I don't want to be a historian at all.

There are acres of books about Earps. Whole ranches of books about cowboys. That's not my territory.

There's even a word for the field of study: *Earpiana.* Used in a sentence: *A foremost figure in the field of Earpiana.* He's here with us today, expounding in PowerPoint:

Late afternoon. A cramped back room of the Arizona Historical Society. He ponies up his bonafides. *Been researching since I was seven.* Says *gestalt.* Says *gut feeling. Warluck.* In the Q&A, hands shoot up quick. Men duel, debate *was there another way,* debate why a few white men had to die. *Isn't it true that Earp shot first?*

So what if it is.

Here's what : it's always **LEGEND** versus **TRUTH**. As used on the back of another Old West Tombstone book : *The Truth Behind the Legend. The Legendary Life. Truth Beyond the Myth. The Real Life Story* . . . &et cetera.

To grow up in Arizona is to spectate experts coming to Arizona to tell you the **TRUTH** about Arizona. Writing all myth and no real life, or events but no meaning. Look, there's only room in this room for one of 'em. To grow up a man is to always know who shot first.

So if men are measured by their accuracy, then I'd rather miss by a mile. When a man puts me to his back, tells me to count ten paces, I keep walking until I'm back haunting the cottonwoods. Don't come looking.

I won't invite you out to the ranch for eggs&Earpiana. But for the right price, I'll tour-guide you to ruins where children are raised.

As seen in my book : *the* **TRUTH** *is that the* **MYTH** *is not a dead* **LEGEND**. It's a zombie, cowboy:

“ The declaration ‘we hold these truths to be self-evident, that all men are created equal’ was written by a man who enslaved men he did not consider his equal, and became the

> foundation of a country that incessantly declared its belief in truth and justice while enslaving and oppressing much of its population. ”

That part wasn't in the PowerPoint. Nobody invited Professor Sarah Churchwell. Back out in the lobby, I can still see where they cut *Pioneer* from the name of the Historical Society. There's a ticket booth. A newspaper, a headline, a shooting, a politician's *this is not who we are.*

The Earpist wants us to agree. So I guess that makes me **CLANTON**. He&I step outside. Our spines mingle. You count it off for us —

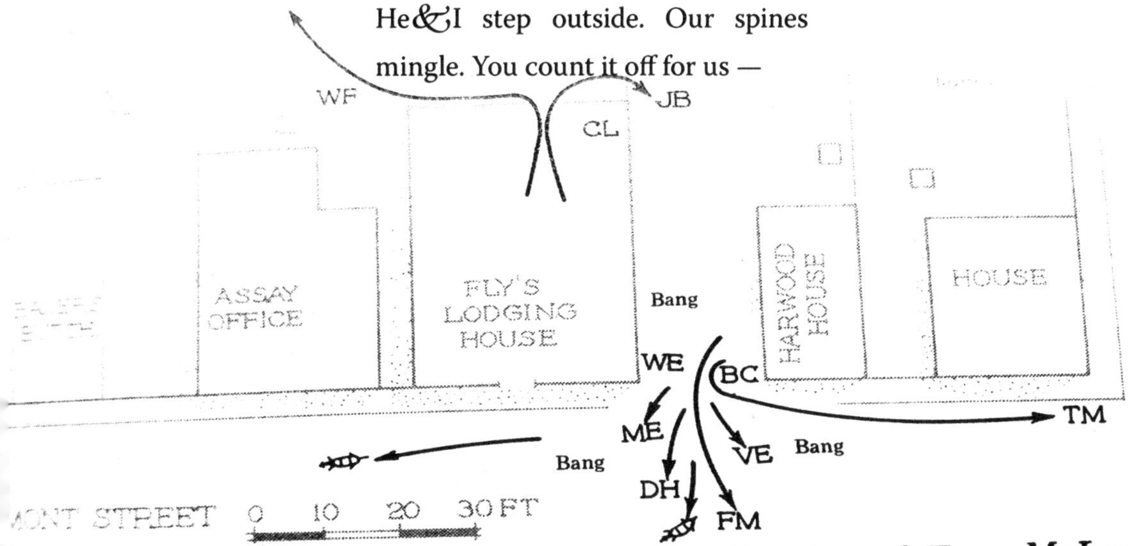

lanton fell dead at the Harwood house. Frank and Tom McLaury led into the street and were hit as they returned the fire. The fight lasted no more than thirty seconds and history was made

The Tombstone Epitaph.

Founded on the Southwestern frontier by John P. Clum, May 1, 1880.

The local edition of The Tombstone Epitaph is published fortnightly by students of the University of Arizona Department of Journalism.

Use of the name is by permission of the owner, Tombstone Epitaph Corporation, publisher of the National Tombstone Epitaph. The Corporation granted permission for use of the name for a local edition of the Tombstone Epitaph on February 2, 1975.

LOCAL EDITION

Editor:	G. Phillip Morago
Managing Editor:	Ann Norton
News Editor:	Douglas McDaniel
Photo Editor:	Jim E. Calle
Production Editor:	Cynthia Dunn
Copy Chief:	Yvonne C. Tost
City Editor:	Steven Graubart
Lifestyle Editor:	Lorri J. Smith
Sports Editor:	Ned Mackey

Epitaph Staff: Frances C. Bobbe, Bruce Jorden III, Victor Morales, Bennet Oreck and Diane Rechel

Phones. 457-3661 in Tombstone and 626-3618 or 626-2561 in Tucson. The Epitaph encourages letters to the editor but reserves the right to edit all contributions to conform to Epitaph style.

Mailing address: The Tombstone Epitaph, Journalism Department, University of Arizona, Tucson, Ariz., 85721.

HISTORIC

Continued from page 3

said.

The new parks office is habitable now, Mr. Phillips said, but added that employees will probably not move across the street to their new quarters until spring or early summer.

LETTER

Dear Editor:

I am writing you in the hopes that you will have the kindness in your heart to place my letter in your newspaper in hopes someone who might be kind to me, will write me back.

I was born in Tombstone. My mother left me when I was four years old, and I haven't heard from her since. I have been living in and out of foster homes all my life.

I am a white male and 24 years old. But when it comes to loneliness, no color or race should stand in the way. I have never felt so lonely in my whole life and so sad. I don't have anyone to write to.

I would appreciate anyone as a pen pal in and around Tombstone who would be thoughtful enough to write to me and share a smile from time to time with a very lonely person. Please write to me.

Thank you for your time in the behalf of me.

Billy Melear

TREASURE
ELEVATION
AND
SPIRITUAL REDEMPTION,
"of course this is all reviled but then, thats the rush
MAGICAL LAWS.
AND AN
All-Arizona Horror-Western Production

Stories of haunted houses abound in town. The latest one concerns a member of the Tombstone Repertory Company, Inc. who put a tape recorder in Schieffelin Hall overnight. Sounds of footsteps and creaking and shutting doors were heard on the tape the next day.

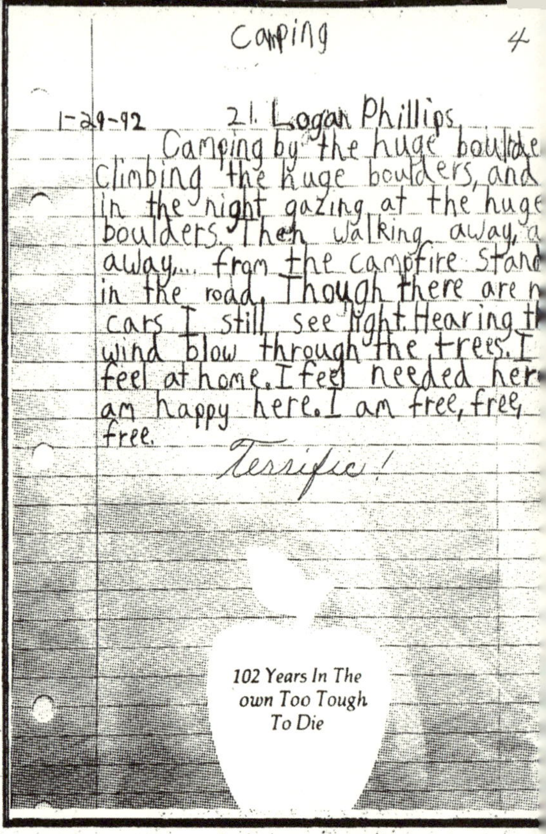

Camping 4

1-29-92 21. Logan Phillips

Camping by the huge boulde[rs] climbing the huge boulders, and in the night gazing at the huge boulders. Then walking away, a[way] away... from the campfire stand[ing] in the road. Though there are n[o] cars I still see light. Hearing th[e] wind blow through the trees. I feel at home. I feel needed her[e]. [I] am happy here. I am free, free, free.

Terrific!

102 Years In The [T]own Too Tough To Die

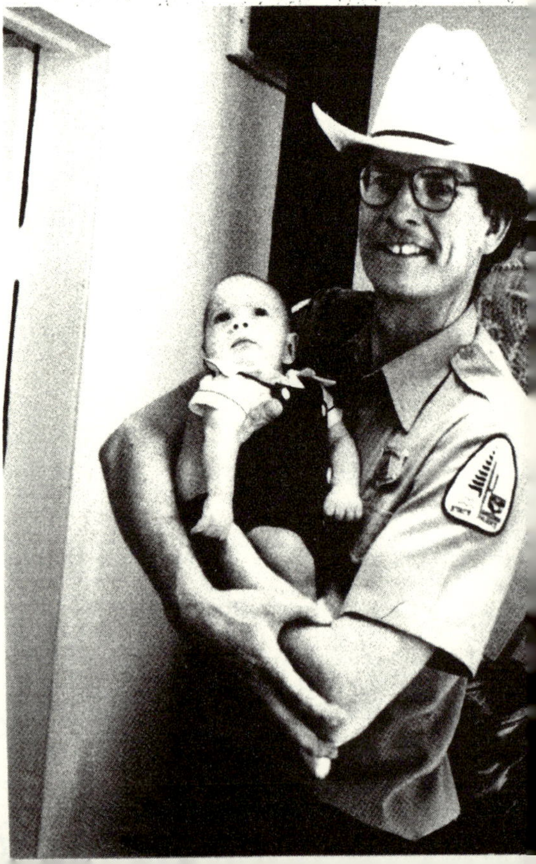

Youngmother&Youngfather   cashed out of Tucson
bought in a busted town   a set of almost ruins on

OLD CHARLESTON ROAD

a woodhouse &a mudhouse   both sliding down an arroyo
filled with historic trash   glittered purple glass
couldn't leave a marble on the kitchen table   without it rolling off

to the corner of the room   something in the earth pulling
everybody to it   some metal   some law   some greed
down there   buried in the mineral rights

but understand   even Youngfather was   prospecting prospects   looking
to strike it   middle class   assay a paycheck   &see what panned out
he took a job   at the **COURTHOUSE MUSEUM**

because story   was the onlything   that paid anything
while over at the **O.K. CORRAL**   **EARP** still circled
in **GUNFIGHTS GUNFIGHTS GUNFIGHTS** for

another tarnation of tourists   gawking a shooting
gobbling a steak   ogling sepia   performing a postcard
but look   Youngmother&Youngfather   tried forever before Babyme

everything was just bust   back before their little baby boom
&then they did what new parents do :   repeated   what they'd been told
&acted out the roles of the drama   they found themselves in

pretended to know   before they knew   &learned to know
what they felt   they should've already known
put Babyme on the back of a bike   &rode :

down **TOUGHNUT**   to the **COURTHOUSE MUSEUM**
over to **ALLEN**   past the **BIRD CAGE THEATRE**
&on back to the **MUDHOUSE**   in circles&circles

{ the sun **SETS**

shooting shimmer
through bruised sky

rain curtains   closing }

was Youngfather an **EARP**   was Youngmother a **BIRD CAGE**
will I ever **RINGO**   is it all courthouse   or all dice-throw
was I born **O.K.**   a toughnut   was I born **O.K.**   a huckleberry

a lucky cuss   another bird   of passage   all shuffled up
a bird-of-paradise   yellow-lipped   epigraphed in caliche
was I boy   born sixshooters   for fingers

born deputized   a silver mine   director's chair   marquee-marked man
already **EARP**ed in iteration   born prospected &claimed acacia
scarlet-corralled heir   circling cyclical highnoon   practicing the die-slow

understand
I could've been born in a pit mine   I could've been born a saguaro scar **O.K.**
born in a single-wide   acre of asphalt   under the **SUPERSTITIONS**

born in another tongue   querencia fronteriza   ocotillo espina **SONORA**
born born   nacido **O.K.**   but instead   born into florescent efflorescence
of a Cochise County hospital   &a rash   of **GUNFIGHTS**

was it **18** or **19**   born in **’83** or in **’83**   **TOMBSTONE**   tell me
what’s a century   when learning   to walk
what’s a horse   bound to springs   to do
but gallop   toy horse squeak   gallop gallop
surrounded by sunsets   sunset sunset

flooded mineshaft   what’s your version of events   was I foolish gold
thinking I could get away   from this mannequin masculinity
this Möbius reenactment   this mutoscope gunfight ?

truth is I was born   a Gambel’s quail   plumed of last light
alive   a vociferous Fouquieria   florescence in my flourish

{ the sun **SETS**
leaving the sky smalt

punctuated by the first twinkling
bullet holes

from pistols pointed up

holding up
the night }

DUST

SUCKED TO

SALIVA

TURNS TO

ADOBE SLOP THEN

HARDENS

A MUDHOUSE

OF THE MOUTH

A SET

OF FIRST

WORDS

SUN

FINGERS BEAM

THROUGH

ARIZONA LIVE OAK

LEAVES

PIERCING I

CRY

LAUGH

FIRST MEMORY

GUNFIGHTS
GUNFIGHTS
GUNFIGHTS

Welcome to Tombstone
AND BOOTHILL GRAVEYARD.
BURIED HERE. ARE THE REMAINS OF
TOM McLOWERY - FRANK McLOWERY AND BILLIE CLANTON
KILLED IN EARP-CLANTON BATTLE SEPT. 26TH. 1881
DAN DOWD. RED SAMPLE. TEX HOWARD. BILL DeLANEY AND DAN KELLY
HANGED LEGALEY BY J.E.WARD. SHERIFF. FOR THE BISBEE MASSACRE. MAR. 8TH 1884
JOHN HEATH
LYNCHED BY BISBEE MOB. FEB. 22ND. 1884
M. R. PEEL
MURDERED IN CHARLESTON. MARCH. 8TH. 1882.
BILLY GROUNDS. "DUTCH" ANNIE. INDIAN BILL. PAT LYNCH. BILLY KINSMAN. BLACK JACK. BRADY BROTHERS
MIKE NOONAN. CHINA MARY. JOHN HICKS.

COME see a quickdraw

faster than you read the words

GUNFIGHTS
GUNFIGHTS
GUNFIGHTS

pistol-twirlin

NINE O'CLOCK

HIGHNOON

THREE O'CLOCK

daily

&

the authentic cowboy

poetry of **BOOTHILL** :

HERE LIES LESTER MOORE

4 SLUGS FROM A 44

NO LES NO MORE

read it for yourself

QUICK *!*

well come on over folks
first things first it's pronounced *urp*
but it's spelled **EARP** —

not everything is as it ears
or hears how it writes

WELCOME

here history comes alive
dead or alive **YES**
real lively livid history see

GUNFIGHTS
GUNFIGHTS
GUNFIGHTS

HEAR how men died
back when men were men were men

how bullets wound
&came all the way round

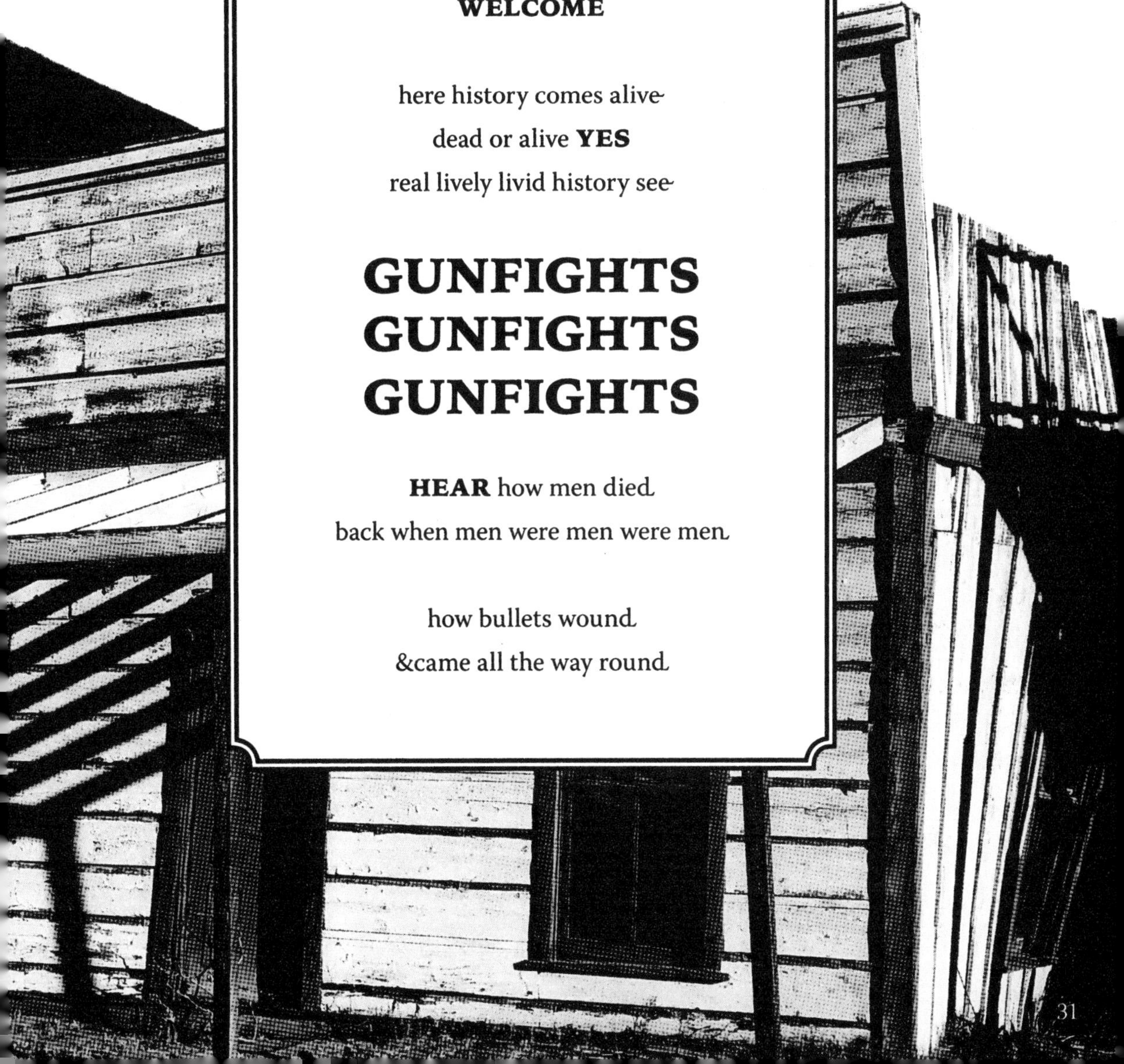

can't say I know   how to unbuckaroo el vaquero
aun hablando español y así   it ain't a quick assay
to sort *vámanos* from *vamoose*   it's been aggregate
but cowboys were Black&Mexican   until they hit the silver screen
y la Época de Oro was all charro too   overexposed celluloid
black&white   more white than black   what's new ?

not this : the Cochise County sheriff   wearing his ten-gallon
cameras rolling   reading the script   claiming invasion
not this : the rich politician   telling us to hate the poor
not this : the Border Patrol agent   on horseback
waving whips at Black Haitians   on the riverbank
what century is this anyway ?   the twenty-first

but where're *you* from ?   the words *colorado condado cochise corral*
nevada santa cruz sierra vista   ¿ y yo qué ?   ¿ cómo es que
I ain't entered the poem yet   tomando por dado   que hablo así
talking as if I wasn't part of it ?   well   I want to tell you
this is just how we talk   in **TOMBSTONE ARIZONA**   except it ain't
yo luchaba pa esta lengua   trying to hear past   what I was told

y aun así   it ain't only me   the horizon reseeds   as I write my horse
toward destination   &there ain't no horse   ain't no absolution
just Kidme   at the kitchen table   spinning spirograph
tangle to pattern   speak&spell   borderlands AM radio
accordions swirling from static   writing down in messy black pen
every Spanish word he could think of   *desesperado*   to *desperado*

at the **MUSEUM** Kidme kerplunks a coin into the ol' **MUTOSCOPE**
puts face to viewer cranks the handle gears turn fotos flip flip
flipflipflip so fast pictures motion an early motion picture
the scene is a **GUNFIGHT** big surprise when the end comes
the bodies pop back up &gunsmoke each other again
&again until the quarter runs out &the audience goes broke

&Kidme learns from the **EXHIBITS** whether he understands them or not :
cowboy : impulsive individual who through a show of force attempts
to resolve a conflict to corral is to gain control of anything Apache :
from the Zuni ápachu *'enemy' famous for their bellicose behavior*
inextricably linked in the popular mind with the cowboy

&killer cowboys are how the stakes are set in *Tombstone* (**1993**)
the opening scene tropes massacre of a Mexican wedding
to say **LOOK** these cowboys are **BAD** they even shoot the padre
&drag the bride into darkness while Kidme watches big screen
learning to see disposable brown characters a blockbuster &no Black actors
renegade from *renegado* *cinch* from *cincho* *nada* from *nothing*

so what's a **YEEEEEHAW** to a **HOWDY DO** ? what's a **HOoOME** home
on the **RANGE** ? what's a hobby rancher shooting a migrant in the back
years after writing a shitty novel about a hero rancher shooting a Mexican ?
a headline ripped from a drama a historama a rodeo break ?
whiteness miraged as truth&consequence ? a vacated vacada ?
a cinch a steal a snitch a 'stache a freeholy in the ol' switcheroo ?

fuck this it ain't where I'm from except yes it absolutely is

RUSTED SAFE

HALF BURIED IN SILT

FLOODPLAIN RIVERBOTTOM

NOBODY CLAIMS TO KNOW

WHO INHERITED WHAT FROM WHO

WHERE HOW IT GOT THERE

WHOSE
HEIST + WAGON

WHOSE
ROPE + IDEA

WEALTH STRUNG OUT

ALONG STEEL RAILROAD

TRACKS TANGLED AROUND COTTONWOOD

AFTER
THE FLOODRUSH
AFTER
THE BONANZA

SHIFTING SANDS
OK

CROOKED LINES
OK

COWBOYS&   ! **COWBOYS**&   !

on the playground sand   Huachuca Mountain Elementary
the games we played   were always about pursuit&ambush
catching&cycles   of retribution   nobody had to teach Kidme

how to roll his **R**s   nor the games   he played
kids know   before they know   who is **US** and who is **THEM**
kids know   playground a theater   where history is inherited

LOOK if Kidme holds his hands like **THIS**   they're a pair of six-guns
if Kidme holds his hands like **THIS**   they're a gatling gun
Kidme learns to roll his **R**s   by making his mouth   a gatling gun

COWBOYS&   ! **COWBOYS**&   !

at the Main Gate of Fort Huachuca   the cavalry outpost   a baby-faced soldier
waves through   Youngfather's white Isuzu truck   driving Kidme
to visit the **MUSEUM**   his job   building exhibits with material he was given

the museum's archive is the old backstage   of an integrated theater   there
Youngfather shows&tells Kidme   hands him an obsidian chipped arrow tip
a tool turned artifact   an arm of resistance turned army trophy

the material the story : **THEY** were here   &now they're **NOT**
Kidme left to wonder how&why   to wonder   maybe they deserved it
— not then knowing   **THEY**   not then knowing   **IT**

COWBOYS &   **!**   **COWBOYS &**   **!**

I didn't start to see till Kidme   was also history :
land as void   once peopled   empty-mapped
makes the mind another gun   with silencer

settler imaginary   more dangerous   than imaginary settlers   or warriors
Kidme saw   as shadows stalking the ridgeline   watching him closely
Kidme didn't need to imagine his position   running through the tall grass

he already knew   side choosing   &revenge revenge revenge
rifle stocks between boulders   { &later deathrays from mountaintops —
I'm still learning   what pretending can do }

COWBOYS &   **!**   **COWBOYS &**   **!**

the games we played were filled with
                &
land acknowledgments are filled with

violent silence   exclamated the world   &Kidme made me
so this is how   a kid could still settle   how
thinking of history as history is useless

no — not useless
a very particular use
Kidme was born into

realistic

GUNFIGHTS GUNFIGHTS GUNFIGHTS

relic

from back when a mass shooting
could still make the **NEWS** *!*

do you want to know   what really happened *?*   I was there that day
back in **'99**   barely **SIXTEEN** at **BUENA HIGH**   **APRIL 20th** &I was so high
the day of the first school shooting   hallway swarmed queasy   Columbine

had been   name of mom's favorite flower   then every classroom **CNN**ed
the first kids to be killed   on cable   while I puked into toilet water splash
to the sound of sirens   we couldn't tell ourselves   what was happening exactly

no phones then   just lip rumor &handdrawn notes   close enough
I felt the danger   like it was about to happen to me   my first bad trip
but not my last   I didn't know   I was at the beginning of a history

nothing about Buena was especially good   except some friends   from circles
with no overlap   my goth friends from Poetry Club   said teachers&bullies
were harassing them   about having guns now   I don't think I mocked them

but can imagine I might've   put the blame   where I was told to
like a patriot   I was just a kid   risking it all in the parking lot after school
heart galloping   watching a fist smash a nose   into a viscous ruddy rose

TEENME   from the edge of the action he cheered   *don't be a pussy!*
TEENME   so damn quick   to draw his tongue
on the side of every violence   he was trying to save himself from

Hey There Coyboy

I either want to fight him or *be* him and I can't tell which.

Which says a lot about my relationship with this place.

I either want to fight him or fuck him and I couldn't tell you which.

And doesn't that just sum up my experience with sex education.

I've had crushes on men for a hundred years. For forever. Why not? Men are beautiful. Or they can be. When the light's just right.

So am I queer?

Aren't we all?

I mean, straight vs. queer is just another gunfight, right? Another line on the map I was born into.

Honestly I didn't know anyone who was out until I moved away from Cochise County. I was 18 or 19. I've always been a late bloomer.

But in Cochise County, we fight or we fuck.

We fear our desire, and so we fight it. We fight those who desire openly. To prove ourselves.

But it's jealousy. It's desire.

In high school, boymen face off, in each others' faces, face-to-face. Nose-to-nose. Cheek-to-cheek. We're about to cry. We're surrounded on all sides by the crowd, or we're in the crowd. We're about to beat the living shit out of each other.

The way I've heard it told, it's always been vigilantes&vigilettes. But at least we've made progress. Gunfighters had to start back-to-back &walk ten paces before they were even allowed to look at each other at highnoon.

Isn't this all obvious?

> "The first act of violence that patriarchy demands of males is not violence toward women. Instead patriarchy demands of all males that they engage in acts of psychic self-mutilation, that they kill off the emotional parts of themselves. If an individual is not successful in emotionally crippling himself, he can count on patriarchal men to enact rituals of power that will assault his self-esteem."

Yeah, bell hooks wasn't taught in our high school.

But hasn't this been said before? I mean heartbreak in *Moonlight.* I mean *Brokeback* cliché. No, I mean Burroughs's *The Place of Dead Roads,* Smith&Wessons &throbbing purplish cocks. Homo gangs robbing the coaches in broad daylight, *Outlawed.*

I mean just **LOOK** at him. Sure, he's no Val Kilmer in *Tombstone,* but still he's drinking an **A-1** in Gleeson. Having a smoke outside an adobe bar in a ghost town. Eyebrows practically penciled. Eyes practically shut, they've seen so much sun. Boots worn. Lips in mid-reminisce.

But look. My queerness is like my cowboyness. It's just there. I don't need to always wear my boots to have been born in Tombstone.

So many people I love hold their queerness central to their identities, and I get it, I love it. Be visible and unapologetic and let motherfuckers get cut just *looking*.

But do I get to call myself queer? I mean I'm partner to { a person who also questions the assumptions of being called } a woman, we have kids. I'm a youngfather. I pass. I get a pass. I rarely get called out on the street. Most of the men I've loved were beyond my reach. So just who do I think I am? There's so many lines in the sand.

I don't know what to tell you, other than I want to buy that man a beer. Ask how come he got his picture in the paper. We'll talk about the land. About saguaros because why not? We won't face each other because then we might have to fight. Instead we'll gaze into the hazy mirror behind the bar, glances bouncing between the ornate liquor bottles, the giant odalisque hanging over us. The jukebox will play the right songs at the right times without us having to touch it. The place will be mostly empty. Late late afternoon.

We'll head outside for a smoke, bring our beers out with us. End up climbing to the ridge of a tailings pile to get a better look at the world.

The sun will sink, and our fingers will wind like barbed wire. Fuck the maps. It's **1983** in a ghost town, and we're about to be born.

MIRAGE DRAINS

OFF THE FLATS

FLOODS THE ARROYO

MANKILLING FLASH

LOOK HOW DEATH

SHIMMERS

A SILVERSCREEN

A ROILING RUSH

A FIRST LOVE

I'm laying on what's left of the **WOODHOUSE**   cracked concrete
running up my spine   &every time I come back here   a **GUNFIGHT**
breaks out   mirage rains from the blue sky   makes mud of me
my eyesight from homesite   becomes a kaleidoscope gunsight —

it's real **REAL** *right ? —*   yes a fuckin fake town   a pinche claptrap
all these cap-gunfighters from elsewhere   selling me what I already know
boosters vs. debunkers   ridin bronc or deridin bunco   writin real clunkers

that chalky meth of myth   crusty dusticle   hung under the mustaches
these tinhorn tenderfeet   snakekillers bluff real big —   lemme **EARP** 'em
neck massage   from a telegraph pole   give 'em the news &let headlines holler

GIVE UP YOUR ARMS OR THROW UP YOUR HANDS *!*
MURDERED ON THE STREETS OF TOMBSTONE *!*
SHOT BY FLY *!* **LAST SHOW** *!* **SEE 'EM DIE** *!*

posthumous postcard   sanguinary affray   vermilion simulacra
some boom goon   gone all buffoon   bemoanin boon gone moot
ergo the argot   a snowbird shootist   blood-smear all cochineal

I reckon a way to unsay 'em all   so I get up   to get even
but this drab slab   is the only place I can stand   to visit
in this varnished two-bit town   when I come down
only to ride on back to **TUCSON**   the vain big city where

{ the sun **SETS**
freeway glare }

LISTEN !

that writer

he's not an actor

or even a reenactor

he's a goddamn **FAKE**

didn't even grow up in

TOMBSTONE !

don't believe his book

it's not even really about

TOMBSTONE !

why he never

even owned a **GUN** ! that

GUNFLIGHT
GUNFUSS
GUNFLIRT

if he has complaints

let him come face me

in the meantime

COME SEE

the **REAL** thing !

COME SEE this **FAMILY**

recovering **CATHOLICS** now **PARENTING**
aided only by love an electric can opener
&residual **LSD** in their spines

YES *!* the **REAL** old **80s**
raising up **BABY** to be a **BOY** in **TOMBSTONE**

COME SPECTACLE Youngmother
working a **SCHOOLHOUSE**
WITNESS Youngfather
working a **COURTHOUSE**

LOOK *!* through a man as **PRISM** : **KIDDAD**
into a **YOUNGFATHER** into an **OLDDAD**
living his history with your very eyes

BEHOLD *!* how a man can
be so close&so far from a son
a reenactment of how he himself was **RAISED**
deeply loving yet **HAUNTED** in the arid air
of a uniquely **MASCULINE SILENCE**
— for as the schoolhouse tells us
energy is neither created nor destroyed

but passed down generations
&that's a **FACT** —

EYE-WITNESS how
for **YOUNGFATHER** it becomes all the **RAGE**

SEE him
SMASH against the earth
RIP tin from a roof
BREAK a bicycle chain

— &yes there must be a receiver of that energy
RAGE must be felt
for if a **RAGE** falls alone in the desert
is it truly **RAGE** ? —

get your front-row seats
to the **SPANKING** of **CHILDREN**

— mind you it was not **WRONG**
it was the **80s** ! —

All-Arizona Horror-Western

Did you ever see *Natas : The Reflection* (**1986**)? Kidme neither. B-grade horror wasn't what Youngmom liked him to see. The film's guest star: Nino Cochise, who told reporters he was 109 and the son of Taza, leader of a Chiricahua band of Apaches. Taza's people were told that while taken on a trip to see Washington, D.C., in **1876**, Taza died of pneumonia.

Did you ever see *Taza, Son of Cochise* (**1954**)? In **2000** Teenme wore a T-shirt that said **COCHISE** across the chest. Cochise College was where he took calculus to be able to graduate high school and escape to Northern Arizona University. Both Teenme&Kidme loved being outside, loved camping, loved the Dragoon Mountains. The Dragoons — Cochise's stronghold — were kept by the Chiricahua through a treaty signed in **1872**. Did you ever see *Broken Arrow* (**1950**)? Cochise was played by an actor in redface, just like in *Taza*. Nino wasn't even Apache, just a no-count early reenactor in **1950s** Tombstone, lost in his lore. What's worse : his faking or those who sold his story? Nino never saw *Natas*, he died in **1984** in the same hospital where Babyme was born. He's buried overlooking the Dragoons.

How about *The Battle at Apache Pass* (**1952**)? Cochise died in **1874**. In **'76** the Chiricahua were forced out of the Dragoons by the U.S. Army & John P. Clum — later the publisher of *The Epitaph*. Then it wasn't long before the mining and cattle booms began.

Kiddad probably saw all these movies. Kidme was born on that land. History is what he was shown and all the horror he wasn't.

ARSAL- A few of Wes Flowers' actors kicking up the dust on Allen Street. (photo by Linda Schutte)

OY OLD WEST

hatterhand' Rides Again

— Citizen Photo by Dan Tortorell

Teaching Some Tenderfeet

How to handle a shooting iron is explained by Steve Eastin, Old Tucson actor, to some U.S. Travel Service visitors. From left, Jack H. Richardson, USTS

They are on a 6,500-mile fly- g trip which the USTS calls The Selling of America, 71." It's aim is promoting avel by foreign tourists to e United States. The three- ur visit here consisted of a s trip to San Xavier Mission d Old Tucson.

Tucson was included on the ross-the-nation trip because is "the epitome of the Old est," he said.

Observations by members of e group, related in inter- ews by the Tucson Daily itizen, included:

—Kevin Rafferty, reporter ith the Financial Times in ndon, giving his impres- ons of Old Tucson: "I ought the gunfight was a tle contrived, but I suppose ey do it so often. The street d buildings are very im- ressive."

—Glennys Bell, reporter ith the National Times in ydney, Australia: "We were ought up on the West as much as you were. To see it is very exciting. Those hills — I could just imagine cowboys rounding a bend. And to see Old Tucson as three-dimensional, not just false fronts, was wonderful."

—Regh: "You have a lot going for you, because all Germans have an inkling this part must be the real America. I think there is a potential for including dude ranches here in tours for Germans."

—Knuth said his outstanding impression during the visit here was "the great joke of the gunfight." He added the Tucson area seemed "a good place to make a vacation."

—Hubert de Segonzac, reporter-photographer for Paris-Match magazine: "One thing it looks like at first, it isn't. I know well the Sahara, and this is not desert like that. It is like a high plateau in Algeria. I was surprised to see the wide etendue (expanse) of the town."

HELLDORADO

Cast For Helldorado Comes Under Fire From Locals

Concerned with the authenticity and heritage of Helldorado, some Tombstonians have expressed dissatisfaction with this year's Helldorado cast, claiming most of the actors have lived in Tombstone only five years.

Tony Russell, of Benson, deputy director of Helldorado, said it is true that many of the cast members are newcomers, but that none of the locals ever try out for the production. "This town is best at criticism, but as far as action goes, there's little help," Russell said.

He added that the cast has only a short time to tell a story, so they must condense it. "If you want authenticity, you'd have people watching for 30 days because it's a story," Russell said.

Russell, a member of the Screen Actors Guild who has worked with both the Wild Bunch and the Vigilantes, said if he makes people laugh through the skits then he's accomplished what he set out to do. "I want to make you laugh, entertain you. I want people to walk away and say 'God, that was funny.' "

Russell challenged locals who are upset with the authenticity. "If they want authenticity, then let us set up props along the store fronts and give us a budget to work with."

Richard Baldenegro, a Tombstone native and director of Helldorado, answered the dissatisfied locals by saying the Helldorado cast tryouts are open, but that no Tombstonians ever show up.

"They're greedy people, they only want it if there's something in it for them," Baldenegro said, adding "if they have complaints, let them face me with them."

Helldorado, advertised as "a true to life reproduction of Tombstone's rip-roaring days," begins Oct. 17.

By M'Liss Christian
Epitaph Staff

TUCSON (AP) — A local high school teacher has announced he will seek the democratic nomination for governor.

Steve Eastin, 26, said he thinks his chances of winning the primary are slim, but that liberal Democrats must be represented in the campaign for governor.

He said he hopes his candidacy will force another democratic hopeful, Raul Castro, to clarify his stand on campaign issues.

Eastin teaches English and minority studies at Amphitheater High School.

Nino Cochise In All-Arizona Horror-Western Production

Nino Cochise, the 109-year-old self-proclaimed grandson of Chief Cochise, relaxes in his Tombstone home. Mr. Cochise recently acted in a movie titled "Natas — The Reflection." He said he worked in Western movies in the early days of film. Mr. Cochise said his last job was as Indian technical advisor for the television show "High Chapparal." (Photo by Ned Mackey)

AN ARIA AT THIS CRISIS WOULD BE FATAL

STANDING on a hill near the San Pedro River, I can just make out a jagged outline on a bluff below me, broken teeth backlit by sunrise.

I cut downslope through the scrub, wait until I hear no cars, then run across Charleston Road, hop a fence, unsure if I'm trespassing. In any case, I don't like to be seen. I follow the sandy curves of an arroyo past a tailings pile and over slack barbed wire and suddenly I'm close enough to read a sign: **BRUNCKOW 1858**. *Do you have any idea how many murders happened there?* Olddad will ask me later. *Whoever came through killed whoever was already there &took it over, threw the bodies to the desert to be devoured by coyotes and rot.* A long tradition in Cochise County. *Not to mention the Apaches*, Olddad adds.

I peek over the decayed adobe and right there in the ruin is a dead coyote, curled up in the shadow, bared teeth, eyes half collapsed black orbs, and I stare into them unmoving I can't break the gaze standing on dirt once bricks my thoughts become indecipherable unreadable I lose the narrative into the scrub The dead coyote still furred untouched by everything except wind &sun &moon &nights &days &weeks &centuries of being dead before these brief moments to &wander &not know &what is it exactly that I'm doing out here standing still over a dead animal, the road so close and everything in me so far away from anyone else which is [illegible] get [illegible] so far out [illegible] might [illegible] I am learning to [illegible] ss as [illegible] I can [illegible] look [illegible] broken teeth [illegible] few [illegible] copypasta [illegible] it a [illegible] Not to [illegible] es, I am learning to [illegible] copypasta copy [illegible] cates itself and [illegible] have [illegible] cheat to [illegible] see this like th [illegible] stem based [illegible] creepypasta [illegible] answers o [illegible]

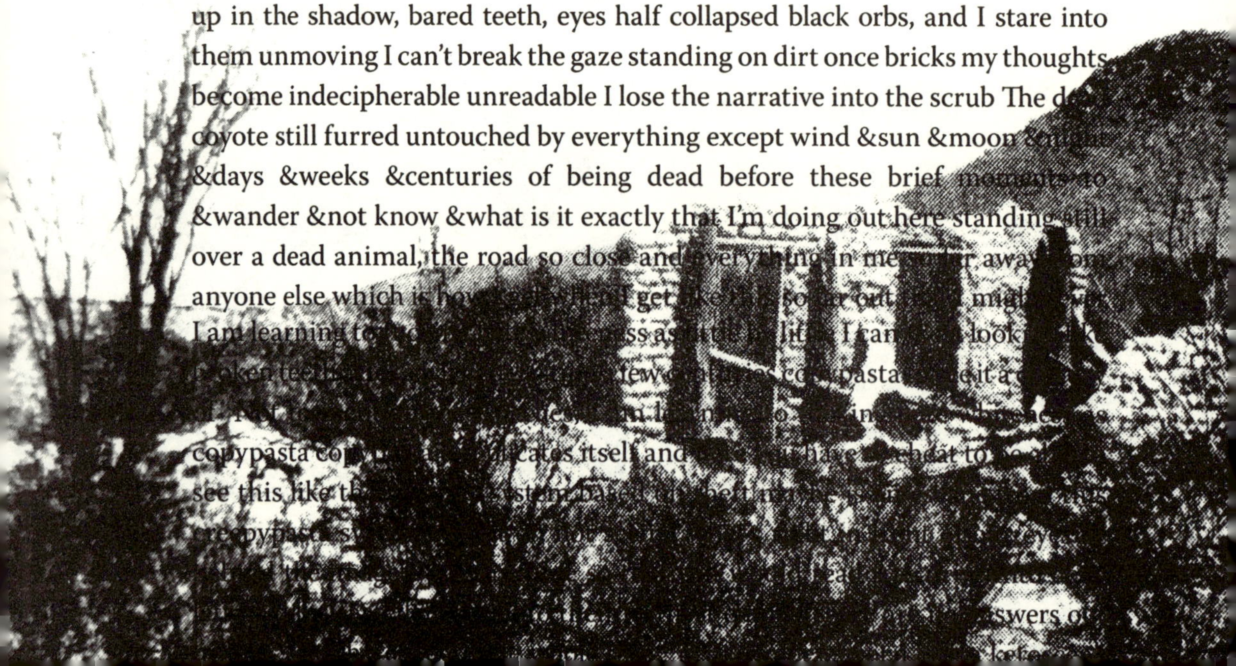

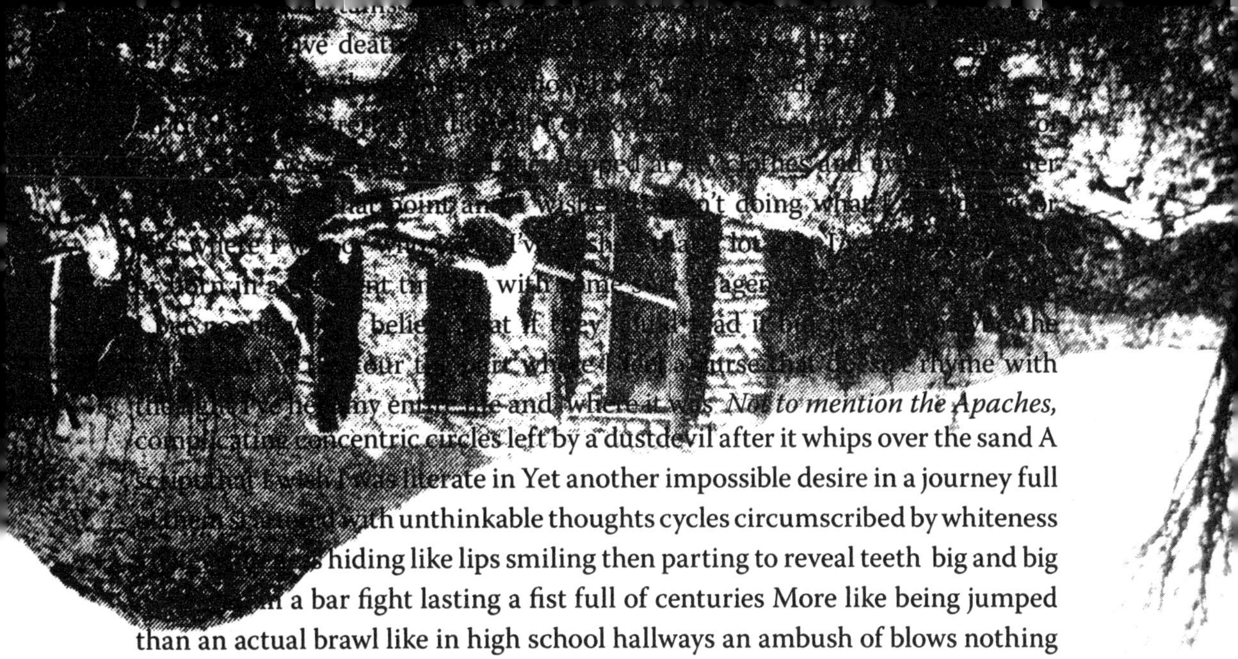

[illegible] *Not to mention the Apaches,* complicating concentric circles left by a dustdevil after it whips over the sand A script that I wish I was literate in Yet another impossible desire in a journey full [illegible] with unthinkable thoughts cycles circumscribed by whiteness [illegible] hiding like lips smiling then parting to reveal teeth big and big [illegible] a bar fight lasting a fist full of centuries More like being jumped than an actual brawl like in high school hallways an ambush of blows nothing to do but curl up &take it the price to pay for what exactly a momentary high of adrenaline&belonging easily flipped in the next moment Youngfather's distance a souvenir bought for him by his father back when walking **50s** Tombstone a raccoon tail hanging down his nape smallest circles of gunpowder all in a tight roll loosed only in explosions *not to mention the Apaches* who did I displace to be here Was never taught to see my Irish-Slavic family as settlers couldn't see colonization as a constant I was born in the middle of all this history everyone had died before I got here Born in another century of gunfights &what I have are poems one word in front of the other not a straight shooter not plainspoken not not guilty definitely dolorem ipsum in the emergency of history Another century another genocide Born curled in the shadow &ambushed by whiteness but who cares unless I survive it still whole &write collapse without enacting another goddamn spectacle of myself But all I was taught was how to spectate &you know who's really lost in this desert Hint not me There are families out here eroding right now &all I do is write&write&write &it's not enough Born in borderlands born in cursed **AMERICA** told not to **NOTICE** or **TRESPASS** nor **TAKE NOTE** I'm not repeating myself I'm inviting **YOU READER** to the next showing trying at an honest living but that's impossible impassable scrambling thorns If truth is a myth and myth is a map what's me lost loving this land slathered in murder Standing over a mineshaft rotten exhalation of infinite pit I want you to understand you've been wandering on unstable ground for as long as you've been following me out here breathing this air The weight of a single question mark could be enough to cause the rotted trusses below us to collapse An ode could do it Certainly an elegy An aria at this crisis would be fatal No singing No more learning to walk I dare you look deeper into my bottomless eyes &inhale with me this heavy dust

PHOENIX
ASSAY
OFFICE

at work in the **COURTHOUSE MUSEUM**   Youngfather reaches into the dark
into the dirt under floorboards   — somewhere someone hasn't touched
since the restoration in the **50s** — there   he finds a beer can

on his lunch break   Youngfather rides   over dirt
out **MIDDLEMARCH ROAD** or some nameless track
bladed white washboard   out toward the Dragoons

{ some great pressure building }

for Youngfather   steeleye Irishman

{ inside him   still burning }

any movement easier than sitting still   so

{ in his firebox   so he pushes himself to go }

out amid thickets of shindagger agave   acres of thorn-tipped clones

his corliss chest   pushes legs   pistons pedals
locomotive spin&spin&spin   fat tires on his steel schwinn
turning the songs stuck in his head   blowing off steam

{ toward the softest parts of himself }

riding   on crumbled quartz   over the next rise

{ his past boiling   then cooling to condensate   running from his skin }

past live oak   pink granite   heavy ethereal   he sweats

{ today he rides   harder than yesterday   everyday }

like a man getting away from something   I can't bring myself to imagine

later after work   Youngfather puts the can
— **A-1**   Arizona pilsner   metal still thick —
on the mantel   of our **MUDHOUSE**

WELCOME to the

GUNFIGHT

and thank you for takin time out of your story
to see our Own Too Tough To Die

I hope to do it justice   and to make it worth the price
you paid   be this your first reenactment
or you've had a century full already

before we begin : this performance does include punctuation
of pistol blanks   I can't promise men aren't hurt
the entrance doors have closed   there's only one way out

when you're called to quickdraw
please be careful coming down those bleachers
they're almost as old as most things in this town

now sit back relax and enjoy a journey to a time
when the Self was myriad
and History was mired every day :

EXT. - SKELETON CANYON - NIGHT

A sky dripping with stars. Beyond darkened boulders an owl **HOOTS**. A coyote **YIPS**.

KIDME: Sure is dark out here . . . Good thing we got this fire! Wouldn't be camping without a fire, would it?

GROWNME: Sure wouldn't. But you know what this scene is missing? A good story. Do you like ghost stories, Kidme?

KIDME: I mean, I guess. It's not *too* scary, is it?

GROWNME: Well, heck, that's up to you. You remember I was raised rural, right? Out in Cochise County, under the Huachucas, I had my run of the range. Mom would send me out and not expect me back till supper.

So this one morning, the sky was dark. One of those days like we used to have, monsoons rumbling all night, drenching even the sunrise, purple cotton clouds hanging low. Remember? Well, I found myself way out, maybe much farther than I should've been at eleven. I was lost in my imagination, thinking about Dad's stories of Apaches riding through here. I started wandering up an arroyo sunk deep into the grasslands. Above me, mesquite trees lined the sides, roots half exposed by erosion, gnarled and intricate. Dangling like giant twisted threads of a curtain stricken by ash, the only barrier keeping the earth from swallowing me whole. The sand crunching under my feet, I kept on up that arroyo, looking to the sky — I think I knew enough to watch for a flash flood.

Coming around a bend, I saw a barbed-wire fence above me, loose and sagging into the void carved by the downcut of the arroyo. A bent sign with rusted bullet holes :

PELIGRO - INSTALACIÓN MILITAR
DE LOS ESTADOS UNIDOS
BASE BOUNDARY - DO NOT ENTER

I had made it all the way to the edge of Fort Huachuca, and there I was, crossing right under without even understanding why the sign was in Spanish. No one had explained to me why migrants walked through here or what it meant to grow up on the border or what crossing really meant.

About ten paces beyond, I stopped — an uncanny feeling of eyes. The air was completely still. A tiny avalanche ran down the earthen wall. A hum came up all around, like an endless echo of thunder, a vibration that was in me, too. I couldn't move. Then suddenly this wind comes rushing down the arroyo and overtakes me, thick and warm, carrying the smell of a thousand generations of mesquites, rains running to oceans, raining again. Vapor mud! Lush death! A copse of corpses, a thieving corpus! A stampede of formless cavalry, hooves cleaving land and my skin!

I'm held in rapture when — ***BOOM !*** A huge military cargo plane ***ROARS*** over the edge of the ravine, so low I can see the seams in its metal body! Propellers deafening! I fall, cover my head, crushed, dirt in my mouth, the earth quivering —

KIDME: Waitwaitwait — you're telling me that *first* you felt funny, then a *death wind* blew, *then* an Army plane buzzed you, all right after you snuck onto post? All of that happened? *Are you sure?*

GROWNME: Look, it all happened. I remember it all at once, but now that you mention it, maybe each one was staggered and my memory is collapsing.

KIDME: So you're not lying to me, or are you?

GROWNME: I'm telling you what I know to be true. But the more of the world you see, the more it blurs on you, kid. What seemed so separate or unrelated now runs together, like a . . . a roll of photograph film shot twice, double exposed.

KIDME: What's that? I don't get it.

GROWNME: Truth be told, me neither. I've never had a gift for recollection, and I'm ashamed. Names and chronologies erode on me. I get sensations and visions, but I've never remembered like most people.

KIDME: So what did you do? Go on.

GROWNME: I just try to be honest, as best I can. But it's probably why when I tried to write a memoir, I failed. And why I make my living as a poet, not a reporter or politician. I have this sense that —

KIDME: No, not *that!* In the arroyo, with the plane and the muddy wind.

GROWNME: Oh! Well, I dunno. I've told what I remember.

KIDME: Oh come *on!* You can't stop like that, stories have to have some meaning — didn't something happen next? There wasn't even no ghost.

GROWNME: No ghost?

KIDME: Just try to remember what happened next — look, what did you *usually* do when you were scared as a kid?

GROWNME: Well, I would hide. Like most kids. I spent a lot of time hiding. Most times in plain sight. Trying to not stand out.

KIDME: O.K., what did you do while you were hiding?

GROWNME: I read. I wrote — carried a pocket-sized pad even then. I sketched, told myself secrets. Dreamed toward what I didn't have the words for.

KIDME: So is that what you did? Start writing?

GROWNME: Not right then : fear was an asphyxiant. Knew I was somewhere I wasn't sposed to be. It was the same land, but somehow different on that other side of the fence.

KIDME: . . .

GROWNME: Dammit, I *do* remember! You know what I did!? Right when the plane was past, I jumped up! Yanked my capgun from the holster & started **BLASTING** away at it BLAM!BLAM! BLAM

BLAM! BLAM! the whole roll!

BLAM! BLAM!

heyheyhey —
    what're you crying about,
    Kidme?

Tucson's Going Places
THIS WEEK at the Community Center

JULY 18-26
GILBERT & SULLIVAN'S "THE GONDOLIERS"

JULY 18
STEPHEN STILLS

AUGUST 3
RUSSIAN NATIONAL GYMNASTS

HOCKEY SEASON TICKETS NOW ON SALE MAIN BOX OFFICE

FOR TICKET INFORMATION 791-4266
MAIN BOX OFFICE 10-6 M-F • 10-2 SAT.

• EASTSIDE CITY HALL 10-4:30, Mon.-Fri. • EL CON 10-5, Tues.-Sat. • FT. HUACHUCA 12-5:30, Tues.-Sat., 6-8 Fri. • DM M-F 10-4:30 SAVINGS 10-4, Mon.-Thurs. • DIAL-A-TICKET 9-5:30, Mon.-Fri. 882-8626 • SOUTHWEST 10-6 Fri. • EL POPULAR in Nogales Mon.-Sat. 10-5

Tucson Community Center

BROADWAY DINNER THEATRE

SPECIAL SUMMER SUNDAY MATINEE (at 12:15)
DISCOUNT price: $6 (includes buffet dinner show and tax)
Price includes dinner & show — Tues., Wed., Thur., Fri., Sun. $7.55 + tax; Sat. $8.50 + tax

PRESENTS LIVE ON STAGE
"LAST OF THE RED HOT LOVERS"
by Neil Simon
Tucson Blvd. at Broadway

Cocktails 6:30, Buffet Dinner 7-8, Showtime 8:15
For Reservations Call after 10 A.M.
882-0782

STARTS TONIGHT
8:10 P.M.
In the tradition of Shane and High Noon, a new Western Classic is born! BITE THE BULLET

GENE HACKMAN
CANDICE BERGEN JAMES COBURN
BITE THE BULLET
IAN BANNEN JAN-MICHAEL VINCENT
RICHARD BROOKS PG

CO-HIT
6:00 & 10:30
CLINT EASTWOOD
THE EIGER SANCTION (R)

Showcase Cinemas 1 and 2
326-2425 — 3233 E. Speedway

"All-out, unzippered sex comedy, it sets a new high in sophistication and even makes explicit screens look sexier."
Bruce Williamson — PLAYBOY

Naked Came The Stranger

STARTS TONIGHT
Showcase Cinema 2
326-2425
X NO ONE UNDER … ADMITTED
7:50 & …

RALPH'S RANCHO
Wednesday Night Special
ROAST BEEF HASH
HOMEMADE & REALLY GOOD
Served with Bowl of Homemade Soup, Dish of Cole-slaw, and Garlic Toast.
OPEN 11 A.M. DAILY FOR LUNCH
$2.25
Phone 887-1330
4635 N. FLOWING WELLS ROAD

294-9101
APACHE
1600 E. Benson Hwy.
2
$2.00 PER CARLOAD
ELIZABETH TAYLOR
LAURENCE HARVEY
"NIGHT WATCH"
BILLIE WHITELAW
PG

AN ELECTRIFYING MOTION PICTURE
The Reincarnation of Peter Proud

LIVE ON STAGE!
FOOT-STOMPIN', SMASH BROADWAY HIT!

DIAMOND STUDS
THE LIFE OF JESSE JAMES
A SALOON MUSICAL

Wednesdays, Thursdays & Fridays at 7 P.M.
Saturdays at 6 & 9 P.M. • Sundays at 4 & 7 P.M.
on the Air Conditioned Sound Stage.

FUN FOR THE ENTIRE FAMILY FUN

Tickets on sale at Arizona Civic Theatre (793-7648) Doubletree Inn, Hilton Inn, Pueblo Ticket Agency & at the gate.

"A GAS! AN UNADULTERATED DELIGHT. YOU CAN'T KEEP YOUR FEET STILL." Clive Barnes, N.Y. Times

PRICE: $3.95 Includes "Diamond Studs", Movie Tour, Live Gunfights, Dancing before and after performances.

OPEN DAY AND NIGHT
Except Monday & Tuesday Nights

Famous Movie Location
OLD TUCSON
12 miles and 100 years away from town

The Scandalous
CINE-PLAZA THEATRE
Call 882-8882
For Movie Titles
RATED TRIPLE 'X'
Now offering '3' New Features a Week! Running continuously from 9:15 AM to 3 AM daily.
318 E. CONGRESS

EXTRAVAGANZA!
LIMITED OFFER
WE HAVE THE PLACE YOU GO FOR
SINGLE MINGLE DANCE CLUB
Singles welcome over 40
We make it easy for you to Join
CALL
886-8225
For An Appointment
We offer Happy Times

$2.00 PER CAR
294-9101
APACHE
1600 E. Benson Hwy
1
What could be better than The Three Musketeers?
THE FOUR MUSKETEERS
ELLIOTT GOULD
MASH

325-2223
CACTUS
1401 S. Alvernon
Sidney Poitier · Michael Caine
The Wilby Conspiracy
— PLUS — "RETURN TO MACON COUNTY" (PG)

Movie Schedule

APACHE DRIVE-IN
Theater 1: "Don't Open the Window" — 7:30, 11:01; "House that Van…d" (R) — 9:23.
Theater 2: "The Bride" (PG) — 7:30, …; "Blood" (R) — 9:08.
Theater 3: "The Specialist" (R) — …; "Super Chick" (R) — 9:31; "The …est Profession" (R) — 11:06.

BUENA VISTA
Theater 1: "Taxi Driver" (R) — 7:30; …e Parallax View" (R) — 9:35.
Theater 2: "Bad News Bears" (PG) — …, 10.

CACTUS DRIVE-IN
…Dirty Mary, Crazy Larry" (PG) — …, 11:09; "Take a Hard Ride" (PG) — ….

CATALINA
…Against a Crooked Sky" (G) — 1:35, …

CORONADO
"Gable and Lombard" (R) — 3:30, 7:35; "I Will, I Will . . . For Now" (R) — 1:50, 6, 10.

EL DORADO
Theater 1: "All the President's Men" (PG) — 2, 4:30, 7, 9:35.
Theater 2: "One Flew Over the Cuckoo's Nest" (R) — 2:25, 5, 7:30, 10.

MIDWAY DRIVE-IN
"Bed Bunnies" (R) — 7:30, 10:48; "Young Playmates" (R) — 9:23.

MIRACLE DRIVE-IN
"Baby Blue Marine" (PG) — 7:30

RODEO DRIVE-IN
"El Padrecito" — 7:30, 11:30; "Los Canallas" — 10.

CINE AZTECA
"Volver, Volver, Volver" — 6:15, "Quinto Patio" — 8:09.

STEVE McQUEEN
"ON ANY SUNDAY"
"ENDLESS SUMMER"
BOTH IN COLOR

Steve Eastin

Coming Next Week: Wolfgang & GRETCHEN

SINGER, SONGWRITER, ACTOR, GUITARIST
Singing Country Rock and Folk Music
Appearing Nightly 8:30 to 12:30 Monday-Saturday
NO COVER AND NO MINIMUM
1365 W. GRANT ROAD at I-10 • 624-2792
HOLIDAY INN NORTH

Singer-Guitarist
STEVE EASTIN
is now appearing at the
Tucson athletic club
8pm to midnight Friday & Saturday
4220 E. Bellevue

MEXICAN BUFFET
Each Thursday
Night from 6:00 pm to 9:00 pm, brightened by traditional Luminarias at the
Lodge on the Desert
Serving appetizers of Jicama, Chili Con Queso, and Quesadillas with this delicious buffet.
RESERVATIONS SUGGESTED
325-3366
306 N. ALVERNON WAY
Between Broadway and 5th St.

JALORIES
MEXICAN FOOD
CATFISH — SHRIMP
LOBSTER — STEAK
PAN FRIED CHICKEN
S. 4th Ave. at 29th • 882-8660
CALL FOR BANQUETS & SPECIAL PARTIES
DINING ROOM OPEN 11:30 A.M.
OPEN SUNDAYS
LOUNGE OPEN 12:30 P.M.-1 A.M. DAILY

LUNCH SERVED DAILY
DINE & DANCE
FRI. & SAT. EVENINGS TO LIVE MUSIC

4 TUCSON 4
WEEKNITES 7:30 WEEKENDS 7:00
WEST GRANT RD. & INTERSTATE 10 624-9305

GEORGE SEGAL & GOLDIE HAWN in
THE DUCHESS AND THE DIRTWATER FOX
PG
plus "W.W. and the Dixie Dancekings" PG

ACADEMY AWARD WINNER!!!!
JAWS
PG
The Great WALDO PEPPER PG

The Fastest Gun In The West Joins With The Most Brutal Hands In The East!
THE STRANGER AND THE GUNFIGHTER
PG
plus
GENE HACKMAN in "BITE the BULLET" PG

NO-TEL MOTEL
CLOSED CIRCUIT X-RATED MOVIES
COLOR and SOUND
WATERBEDS AVAILABLE
$17.50 All Night
$10.50 for 3 Hrs. Daily
2425 N. Miracle Mile
PHONE
622-9304

Ingmar Bergman's
The MAGIC FLUTE
THE NEW LOFT
504 N FREMONT 624-4981

294-9101
APACHE
1600 E. Benson Hwy.
3 THEATRES
$2.50 PER CAR!
BUTCH CASSIDY AND THE SUNDANCE KID
PAUL NEWMAN
ROBERT REDFORD
KATHARINE ROSS
PG

ACTOR-SINGER!
STEVE EASTIN
appearing
WED., THURS., FRI., SAT. —
9:30 to 12:45
Steve will be remembered as Jesse James in that musical classic — "Diamond Studs"!
STEVE EASTIN
Woody Mercer's Cowboy
RESTAURANT & LOUNGE
4402 North 1st Ave. (at Rillito River)
Phone 888-5891
Featuring — Delicious Cowboy Bar-B-Que Beef, Cowboy Steaks, Bar-B-Que Baby Back Ribs and Chicken, and a Variety of Mexican Specialty Dishes!

SPANISH TRAIL
MOTEL AND RESTAURANT SUPPER C…
South 4th and the Freeway • 624-44…
CLOSING MAY 1st
"ERNIE MENEHUNE & HIS POLYNESIAN REVUE"
SHOWTIMES 8 — 10 — 11:45
(SUNDAYS ONLY 7 — 9 — 11)
WE CATER TO BOWLING PARTIES WEDDING & MEETING ROOMS
SERVING TERRIFIC MEXICAN FOOD DAILY
— 24 HR. COFFEE SHOP SPECIALS —
Seconds on the house Wednesday Only
ITALIAN SPAGHETTI DINNER Incl. Salad $1.…
Seconds on the house Friday Only
FILLET OF RED SNAPPER DINNER Inc. Soup $1.…
OPENING MAY 2nd THE FANTASTIC
"SOUTH PACIFIC EXCHANGE" REVUE

Guard derails 'Jesse James'

Jesse James held up the American Freedom Train night — at least, he tried to.

"This is a holdup," shouted Jesse after Gov. Raul ro finished a speech during ceremonies aboard the 1.

Jesse and his gang of 40 assaulted the train, firing ars as they boarded.

Firing their guitars?

Why, it wasn't really Jesse at all. Just actor Steve in and the cast of "Diamond Studs," the Arizona : Theatre musical.

t seems that Freedom Train officials and the local ntennial commission had cooked up the surprise ery by the comedy troupe.

But it was no laughing matter to Eastin. Nobody ered to tell the train's guards. They promptly ked the star to the ground.

'rouper that he is, Eastin dusted himself off and he the cast launched into a new song — "Somebody ed the Freedom Train."

See related story on page 31

galize pot

tor, the Citizen:

would like to address the following com- ts to all who have been writing in protest of legalization of marijuana.

believe the weed is as harmless as booze, and aspirin. However, recent studies by ous researchers around the country show any of the aforementioned compounds, n used in excess, contributes to deterioration ertain organs in the body. Not a human body, 's body . . . .

think pot should be legalized because its use not infringe upon anyone's rights, like rob- , rape or assault does. It is harmless and ions of persons (not only youth) know this. there are good side effects: perception of uli is magnified and emotions such as under- ding, compassion and warmth come to the ace in men. I just wish the older generations d find something that would make them feel , perceive the beauties of nature and have a and warm passion for other men. But they t.

'e, the young, are the victors even though morals and values are constantly sup- sed. The policy makers fear that if our hap- ss were legalized, the whole political system d be undermined. But then that system was on war, greed and hypocrisy.

ontinue to scoff at our marijuana smoking, le, and we will only smile at you and pity — for you are the losers.

JAY SULLIVAN
1007 W. Prince Road

Pondering proverbs

Editor, the Citizen:

Re: Syndicated columnist William F. Buckley's "Who Killed Everybody?" on the Citizen's editorial page of April 23.

I do wish that Mr. Buckley would ponder this proverb: "We kill to satisfy a fear of becoming what we in our ignorance believe to be impossible."

It seems to me that if there is still no room in the (cities) inn, no room in the fields, no room in the plains for our brothers of different hues and of different faiths, why seek peace? Why bother to educate?

Should we strive for might or those principles of right that are spiritually supreme, or both?

ANTOINETTE FIELDS
516 E. Elm St.

LIMITED ENGAGEMENT!

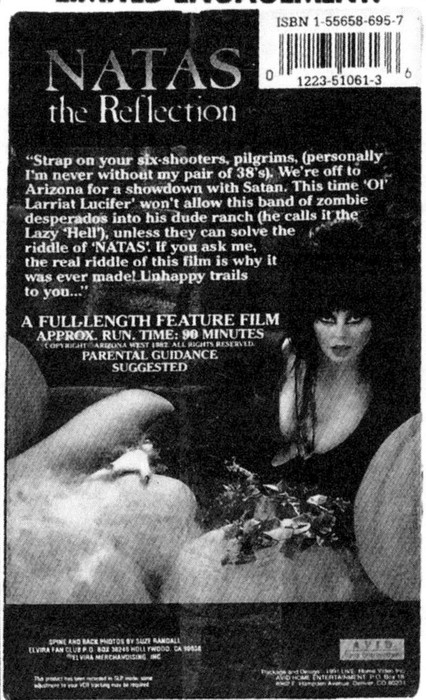

DESERT INN
FREEWAY AT CONGRESS • 624-8151

COCHISE COUNTY

Tombstone, the town with the magic name and a newspaper named the Epitaph, merchandises its past. The few residents of Paradise, regulars or part-timers, hope nobody else moves into their hamlet. At last reports Courtland had one resident — a hermit who kept newcomers at bay with a shotgun.

Other Cochise County history was being made in the early 80s, too. Tombstone and a half-dozen other gold and silver camps boomed and bloomed. Some of them, like Galeyville and Charleston, have almost vanished from the face of the earth and others, like Dos Cabezas, Millville and Russelville are unknown to all but ghost town buffs But Tombstone is solidly established as a monument to the Old West, because of who went there — the Earp brothers, Doc Holliday, Curly Bill Brocious, Russian Bill, the Clantons and McLaurys, Buckskin Frank Leslie, Dr. George Goodfellow, Luke Short, Johnny Ringo, Bat Masterson, Johnny-Behind-The-Deuce and Sheriff John Slaughter. And because of what happened there— mostly the so-called Gunfight at the O. K. Corral, which actually took place in a vacant lot next to Fly's boarding house and in the middle of Fremont Street.

It is ironic that Wyatt Earp, a man-on-the-make who spent only two years in Cochise County, has been recycled into The Frontier Marshal. The honor should have gone to Jeff Davis Milton, in turn a Texas Ranger, deputy sheriff, cowboy, prospector, town marshal, shotgun messenger, Wells Fargo detective and one-man border patrol. He spent most of his long life in Southern Arizona and how many men he had seen through the gunsmoke was something he didn't like to talk about. He was not the type to carve notches in a gun butt and when asked for a body count he would always say, "Well, I never killed a man who didn't need killing."

And now quickly, before I run out of space, here are some of the things to see in Cochise County:

Tombstone, with the old courthouse now a state museum. The Birdcage Theater, Boot Hill, the Crystal Palace Saloon, the Wyatt Earp Museum, etc.,

Cochise Stronghold in the Dragoons.

With the invention of the halftone process in 1880, photographs could finally be reproduced mechanically at the same speed as type, and without the interdicting hand of an artist. The procedure broke the photograph into a series of tiny dots—fewer in the highlights and denser in the shadows—that gave the illusion of tones, or shades of grey. Halftones came into widespread use in the early 1890s.[5] Each of these processes was important to Fly's career as a photojournalist. Initially his photographs were published as beautifully clear steel engravings; eventually they appeared as halftones.

On Location

"You people are never on time," he says, shuffling from his big truck to the combination lock on the rusted cattle gate, leaning heavily on his cane between steps, not looking in my direction. "Didn't expect you so soon. Caught me right about to fix breakfast."

He's dressed in a well-worn Stetson, denim jacket, loose jeans cinched tight with a red flannel shirt half tucked. He's wearing a badge.

The sun is up, but the air is still frozen, that dry Cochise County cold that spends all winter washing down from the snow-covered peaks of the sky islands into the wide shallow valley holding the sliver of the San Pedro River, hidden down in the tangle of naked cottonwoods. A shiver runs through the pale grasslands, through the barbwire.

"Sorry about that," I reply from my side of the fence. "I guess I got an early start leaving Tucson." I use my hips to push my body away from leaning on my car and walk up the rutted dirt road, meeting him at the lock. He's already twiddling the combination, the top of the cane in his armpit. The lock clicks open, and he straightens himself up as best he's able. "Thanks so much. My name is Logan," I say, extending my hand through the still-closed gate.

He squints up at me, the early morning light shining directly into his eyes, which I now see are pale and watery and barely blue behind his glasses. "Hi there. Frank." His bony hand gives a strong grip, but his body is already turning away. "Follow me on up to the top of the hill. You can park up there." He's pulling open the gate as he says these last words, sounding like lifeless lines of a script he's performed too many times.

I'm the stranger that has come to town.

I've interrupted the rhythms of daily life and breakfast making with my fast talk and my car that is not a pickup truck. *Say there stranger, just what the hell do you think you're doing here anyway? You people* — { right hand resting atop the butt of a pistol. }

This is a movie, or it has been, or Frank wishes it was. I'm following his dually up the dirt track, my eyes moving quickly, trying to take it all in : the sticker on the cab's rear window — **COWBOY UP** — the mud flaps, the shadows on the Rincon Mountains, stippled relief of the landscape in low sun. Up ahead, looming larger, is the town of Mescal. Is the town of Tombstone. Is the town of El Dorado. Or El Paso or Dodge City or Sage Creek or Mesilla or Sinola or Pierce, depending on who's doing the writing.

The buildings are coming into view, first a three-story saloon and hotel on the corner, then the long row of building fronts behind it. Even from here, bumping along halfway up the hill, it's clear the town has seen better days. What's left of the second-floor balcony above the saloon is a splintered skeleton.

At the top of the rise, the dirt road widens out into a large clearing. Frank turns his truck, throws it in reverse, and swings quickly into a spot in front of a wood building. Or rather, a decaying façade of a wood building, a single-wide trailer poking out from behind it. I park between Frank and a large sign, many of the letters nearly worn off :

OLD TUCSON STUDIOS

MESCAL

" WORLD FAMOUS MOVIE LOCATION "

GUIDED PHOTO TOURS AVAILABLE

NO WATER, PHONE, RESTROOM,

FOOD OR ELECTRICITY AVAILABLE

NO SMOKING BEYOND THIS POINT

Another sign nailed to the bottom,
looking like it's weathered a quarter century :

~~TEMPORARILY~~

CLOSED TO THE PUBLIC

NO

TRESPASSING

SITE HOST CANNOT

GRANT PERMISSION TO ENTER

"So you're here to do some scouting, huh?"

"Scouting. Well, no. I'm a writer, actually. Just here to have a look around and do some writing. I was born over in Tombstone and grew up outside Sierra Vista. My uncle was an actor. When I was a kid, he invited us out here to see him shoot."

"Is that right. What film was that?"

"I'm not sure . . . I think it was for TV. Late **80s**."

"Huh. Well, come on, I'll show you the place."

Atop the hill, the claptrap buildings of the Mescal set are visible from the freeway if you know what you're looking for. I certainly never knew what I was looking for : in all the thousands of times I've been down I-10 between where I grew up in Cochise County and Tucson, I never saw it. Even after remembering my visit as a kid and wondering about the set in relation to the book I'm writing, I didn't realize the place was so close until an earlier research trip a few months back. In the middle of that long day spent driving back roads on the backside of the Rincons, I had come upon the locked gate and hadn't been able to stop thinking about it since. Even now, knowing where it is, Mescal is liable to disappear, depending on the slice of sun and the shadow of wandering clouds.

I've been arranging this journey for the last few months, waiting for permission to enter "for research." Of course, in my first email I didn't mention that I'm a poet. Nor that my "research" would entail mostly standing on Main Street and staring off into the middle distance.

After a month or so of no reply, an email hit my inbox. I was connected to an enthusiastic publicist named Megan with whom I negotiated the details. Most important, she stressed to me, is that Mescal is a "historic set," and the buildings are dangerous. "You are not to walk on any of the porches nor enter any of the buildings. We'll let the site host, Frank, know that you're coming. If you need to contact him for any reason, call us, and we'll call Frank."

Now I'm standing at the entrance to the saloon, the most grandiose building in town, and Frank is fumbling through his large keychain. I hold the saloon half-door open on its spring-loaded hinges so that Frank can get to the latch on the main door behind it. When he pulls the correct key up, he realizes that the padlock wasn't snapped shut in the first place. "Ah, well," he mutters, then pushes on the large wooden door, but it's stuck. Leaning over, I help push with one hand, and the door scrapes open. Frank hangs his keys back on his belt, rights himself with the help of his cane, and walks in. The half-door squeaks back and forth behind me, stops.

The saloon is beautiful. It's spacious, made of mostly unfinished wood, uneven but seeming solid. There is an ornate bar, chains hanging from the high ceiling where chandeliers could be. There's a broken piano, keys lifted at odd angles. Large windows frame views of the San Pedro Valley, spreading all the way to the Dragoons on the eastern horizon. Light is pouring in, spilling across the rough floorboards. A wide staircase, majestic and dusty, perfect for dramatic entrances or slow, alluring exits. I look up and half expect to lock eyes with some beautiful femme presence, sizing me up, eyes twisting the plot. I want to order a whiskey. This whole place is like something out of a movie, of course. A movie that I've seen many, many times. A movie that I was raised in.

Frank is also standing in the middle of the room, both hands on his cane. He looks around as he speaks.

"This was the last building they built out here, around **'98** or so. I watched them do it, been here since **'97** myself. A lot of shooting back then. They did *Tombstone* around **'91**, most of it was built for that and then just stayed. Over a hundred buildings. Not as many now. Well, anyway. Let me give you my cell number. I need to eat my breakfast. If you need anything, you call me."

Standing in the middle of **MAIN STREET**. No footprints at all in the sand. An errant breeze runs past. Small dust, a swinging sign — **OPEN EVERY** — only half of it left. Red bricks peeling away, showing their fiberglass innards. Wind torn. Sun eaten. The whole front of the **SHERIFF'S OFFICE** has fallen flat, lying face-down in the dirt. Behind it, a weedy mesquite tree. Roofing slats fallen all around. Broken glass. Buildings askew, trapezoids twisting on their

rusted nails. A stronghold of plywood. **METALSMITH**. A ghost town of a fake town. **FRANK'S CAFÉ**. A boom of imagination gone bust. **ASSAY OFFICE**. A decrepit simulation.

My shadow, squared up with me, stretches long and skinny out toward the west, dares me farther into town.

The buildings are varied and all the same in their hollow squalor. Broken windows. Collapsed roofs. The smell of old wood and rodent shit. Wallpaper peeling, rolling itself back up. Another saloon, the bar comically small, made to be filmed from a distance. An architecture made for the lens. A warped pool table. A cloudy mirror. A five-gallon bucket, plastic crumbling. A child-sized wooden coffin leaning in the corner. Tracks in the dust where a mattress has been dragged across the room. Debris, flotsam, and rust.

My boots make loud, satisfying thumps on the boardwalk as I stroll under the porches, sizing the place up, looking for something I recognize. I realize I'm sauntering, the brim of my hat pulled low.

I'm the writer, and this town is *Tombstone.* I was ten years old when the movie came out, released right into the center of my Cochise County childhood. I was primed to love it. I had a hat and boots and holsters and capguns laced with the thick smell of gunpowder. My parents would buy me **CAPS** from Tombstone's tourist-trap gift shops when we'd go back to visit. Rectangular cardboard boxes, red, white &blue. Loaded with reddish paper rolls, dotted at intervals with little pockets of gunpowder that would pop and smoke when the hammers of my little guns hit them. Boy's First Ammo.

My parents probably thought cowboys were harmless, a way of explaining the world to a boy kid.

I walk farther down **MAIN STREET**. There are still no footprints in the dirt, everything raked with wind. Yeah, I recognize that building. I think I do. I recently rewatched *Tombstone* for the first time since I was a teen. With the sound off, I challenged myself to write the whole time, but mostly I couldn't look away. The scenes floated in me like memories, like premonitions. Even the first time I watched, I knew the gunfight was coming — everyone did. But now it all seemed to be saying something so different.

I'm standing at the bar in the second saloon for my second drink of the morning. I know I'm not supposed to be in here, but the doors hang askew and welcome me right in. Suddenly I have a moment of definite recognition: the wallpaper. That's *Tombstone.* On the *Tombstone* DVD extras, a set designer had gushed about it. The attention to detail, the authenticity of the pattern. It is peeling off the plywood like brittle pencil shavings.

I've come to the far end of town, which didn't take long. Out beyond, maybe a half mile distant is another building. An outlier. Another location. It is big and yellow, the paint still vivid against the backdrop of the blue Rincons. **MAIN STREET** becomes a two-track dirt road, becomes a trail looping around the scrubby trees out toward the building. There's probably more to explore in town, but I'm pulled to see the building up close.

I come around a mesquite, and there's the remains of a wagon. A wooden wheel completely broken in half, ribs splayed. I take it as a sign and leave the track, pushing through the grass up to a small rise closer to the building. From here I can see it was surrounded by a large porch, now just a skirt of jumbled lumber. The building's yellow is not paint, but rather exposed yellow-orange foam, the veneer almost completely burned away. Fiberglass twinkling like a filthy geode turned inside out. I can see where the building was made to look worn down, fake bricks exposed through the fake stucco, now all of it slowly sloughing off.

I'm watching the ground now, looking out for rabbit holes and hidden cactus. The earth changes here, becoming more sand, spreading out from a mound. An adobe corral, melting back into the earth. I kneel down, run my fingers over the roughness. Small silica and quartz grains catch the sun. Silent except for whispers of the grass, the sand swims before my eyes. Mountains to boulders to rocks to pebbles to sand. To adobe brick. To sand. An eerie feeling of unwelcome. Unthinking, I look back up at the building.

Immediately my eyes lock into the gaze of a great horned owl, perched in a window frame on the second story. Huge yellow eyes, otherwordly. I am being watched. I have been since I left town. Unmoving, I'm still crouched. Or cowering. We stay like this forever. My legs tingle, then go numb. Wind cuts through me, moves the feathers around the face. The pointed ears articulate : watching, waiting.

Then suddenly the owl disappears into the building, a single silent movement. I fall back on to the sand, shivering in the sun. My legs burn with pins and needles, my body cold from staying so still. Lightheaded, lights dance in my vision. I've been holding my breath.

I'm walking again — in a wide circle, keeping my distance. The west side of this building, the backside, never needed any pretense. Looks like it was always just plywood but now blackened from decades of sunsets.

Out beyond this building, there's still another, a small cabin. Walking out toward it, I tug at the zipper of my jacket. I can't tell if the day is getting warmer or colder as it goes on.

The cabin looks like the rest of the town, except that it's not a front but a full structure. The door is pushed in and so stuck I can't move it, but I'm afraid to really try. I look through the windows and recoil : the place looks like it has just been swept. There's a large stainless steel pot on the floor. A cow skull hanging on the wall. An oxidized bed frame. A peeling hearth blackened from cooking. A rough-hewn table, set with wooden bowls. Three chairs, one turned out toward me. I have the feeling someone is about to speak at any moment. No — there *is* someone speaking, and I can almost hear it. I'm too far in, too far out from town. I back up, one foot behind the other.

Walking back, I concentrate on my feet making contact with the earth. I look up at the high, thin clouds, trace a jet trail slicing the blue at a perfect angle. Down below toward the south, I can make out the freeway, the white boxes of the semitrucks moving across the valley. Every so often, a train whistle comes up from the Southern Pacific, down where the tracks cut through a small freeway-exit town also named Mescal.

C'mon. What is it that you're afraid of here? None of this is real. What's going to happen? The ghost of an actor is going to rise up and grab your shoulder? An actor who died after being shot in the back with a blank? Or no — it'd be a ghost who works as an actor playing a cowboy, right? Lost after some director long ago forgot to yell **CUT** *? Or a real actor, playing the ghost of a dead gunslinger? Man, they're echoes, not sound. Nothing to it. This is all shredded chintz, ragged schmaltz. Fake history. Harmless.*

I'm walking the most direct route back toward the set, cutting across the grass, which takes me near the far corner of the yellow building. I'm trying to stay in my body, find familiar thoughts, but I can feel my heart quickening. *Think about the fiberglass : remember the summer you worked as an electrician, coming home itching from insulation? Think about the script : why didn't Jarre originally write it as good guys vs. bad? Think about Uncle Steve : remember sitting with him in his dressing room, in that RV parked out here?*

Close enough to the building that I could touch it, I stop without thinking to. I freeze and suddenly know what I will see when I look up. Through another window above, the yellow eyes looking directly down into me, perched on shit-streaked rafters. Time flinches again. *No, this is research. You're just watching.*

I move to take a photo, and the huge bird turns, disappearing from the vantage of the window frame. My eyes fall to a hole in the wall, eye level to the raised interior floor. A huge space. Light streaming down from the punctured roof and between the wooden shutters. A grand fireplace, crumbling. Hundreds and hundreds of owl pellets, each the size of a baby's fist. They cover the curling floor, speckled black and white. Many are so old they've fallen apart. Clumps of fur and fragments of pale mouse skeletons everywhere. Scattered skulls and incisors and shoulder blades. Ruined eye sockets. Vertebra. They crunch under my boots as I pull myself up into the building. I walk slowly, trying to avoid the broken floorboards. At the far side, a broken broom leans against the wall. I move farther in. I fill my hands with bones. *Why are you crying?* Above me, the owl.

I'm entering Mescal again when I hear a cough of an old engine, settling into a rough drone. I follow the sound among the buildings, down an alley that runs parallel to **MAIN STREET**. I pass a series of low adobe walls made out of real dirt, then pass the corner of a wooden building and come to the backside of the saloon. There, in a small lot, is a towering generator, mottled orange paint and reeking of diesel. I can't believe the relic is running, so decrepit and surrounded by tinder.

"THEY HAVE ME FIRE IT UP ONCE A WEEK TO KEEP IT WORKING," yelled from right behind me. I jump out of my skin. A skeleton strung with raw nerves like Christmas lights, I wheel around. Frank. Leaning against the far side of the wooden building I just passed, taking in the sun.

"YEAH!" I yell, the only word I can say. He's looking at me now. We stand there. I try to keep my chest from heaving.

He pushes himself up and motions me back to the adobe walls, around a corner that dampens the roar. "Finding what you need out here?"

"Yeah! Uh, I think so, yeah."

"Good. You know there's a lot of history out here, a lot of stories been told."

"Uh, I bet." I gather myself, pull at my skin. "What about that big building out past town? What's that?"

"Well, it's been a lot of things — did you ever see *Christmas Miracle at Sage Creek*? Shot back about twenty years ago. It was the headquarters of the Buffalo Soldiers in that one. And these adobe walls right here? They were the **O.K. CORRAL** in *Tombstone*, where they had the famous gunfight. Doesn't look like much now, but the tourists sure like to see it when they come out here."

"When was the last time anything was shot out here, Frank?"

"Oh, about a month or two ago. A zombie thing. Lots of blood. They had me be in that one too, got my name in the credits. You know I've been in over fifty films out here." Under his white mustache he is smiling for the first time, his face firming up, wrinkles deepening. Standing this close, I have a better look at his badge. **SHERIFF FRANK. MESCAL.** "They said you was a poet, that true?"

I nod. "Yeah, mostly."

"Used to write myself, you know. Prose, don't know what it was. Never did much with it. Guess it all boiled down to 'well, you gotta believe in something, people.'"

"I think that's definitely true."

"So many stories. I don't do much of that now, mostly keep to myself. I used to bust my ass hammering and nailing this place to stay together. A whole bunch of it blew down in a wind storm about a decade ago. Been out here twenty-three years. They don't expect much of me now. Eighty-two years old. It's a miracle I'm still here at all."

The sun has climbed up as high as it can. I'm sitting on the porch of the second saloon — *Tombstone*'s Grand Hotel — leaning against the wall, boots splayed. My blackbook open, writing. Even with Frank's blessing, this doesn't feel like a place I should be. *What do you expect — Megan the publicist suddenly leaping from her hideout yelling* **GOTCHA** *! and hauling you off to movie jail?* An ambush seems both unlikely and imminent.

As a teenager I spent a lot of time trespassing in Cochise County. Ducking into old mines in the Huachucas, throwing parties with Elias at the ends of dirt roads scraped far into the desert, getting high in construction sites with Biskit, making out with Julieta under blankets on the golf course at midnight. Dropping dry ice bombs into porta-potties with Ronnie, watching the blue shit-slurry geyser out of the ventilation pipe. Hiking over iridescent, acid-stained tailings in Bisbee with Cash, glimpsing figures in white ducking into abandoned shafts, or hallucinating. Ditching school to shotgun beers in for-sale houses with Joey. Seeing a pistol for the first time with Julián, realizing I was taking bong rips in a stash house : *no wonder there's no furniture, no wonder the garage is stacked with bundles wrapped in black plastic.* Riding in the car while Rudy — Rudolfo — leans out the window, yelling "wetbacks!!" at migrants walking single file on the shoulder of Highway 92, night air rushing, poisoned. Watching coke replace weed at house parties: "Nah, I don't have any more green, how about some white?" Downing the tequila shots lined up on a bar in Nogales, Sonora, with Benny — Benicio. Stumbling back through the U.S. Port of Entry before dawn. Driving back, blasting rave music CD-Rs to stay awake. Real, real stupid shit. Some of which I got arrested for, most of which I got away with, all of which I survived, somehow. Many others didn't, to some degree or completely. The older I get, the more dead people I know.

I don't want to be seen when I'm trespassing nor own up to all the moments I regret. I don't want to think about the past. But when I'm in Cochise County, I can't help myself. Not the **1880s** but the **1990s**, our own Wild West, just as mythic and misguided. Just trying to find something to do, trying to get laid, looking for fights. We thought power meant the potential to inflict pain. We'd prove we were men, whatever that meant to whoever was watching. All of it a revolving dystopia, still spinning in another century of crisis. A dead-letter future, a third century of "now more than ever."

I've come back to deal with all of it, but I'm getting nowhere. I'd rather go back to writing about the land, the desert and mountains where I used to escape and lie on the ground, feel the earth hold my body. I'd be out "doing some homework for photo class" or telling myself I was just out hiking, but now I can see that's how I was surviving. My art-making started as a way to get away, to abandon the structures and feel my humanness through my senses. Then I spent two decades getting as far away as possible : hitchhiking a night highway in Chiapas. Listening to an old soldier in a rocking chair explain the importance of "socialismo o muerte" in León, Nicaragua. Watching oil tankers ply the horizon while playing guitar on a rock of an island off the Colombian coast. Running out of cash in Cuba, bartering with the languages I spoke. I ran as far away as I could.

I wrote and published an entire book about the contradictions of Arizona without really including myself anywhere in it.

But now I find myself on the movie set where my memories were filmed. I'm doing my best to be honest . . . so I'll admit to making up people's names when writing that abbreviated list of (real) real stupid shit. It feels impossible to reckon with what I can't fully remember or understand. I can tell you the name of every canyon in the Huachucas but not the names of all the people I've had sex with, or the people I've lied to, fought with, betrayed. If forgetting is a gift, I wonder who is the giver?

Anyway, it's not history I want to invest myself in. I don't want to star in the film nor reenact the gunfight. And yet here I am, still surrounded by the mundane architecture of the archetypes that raised me. I learned my history and still I'm doomed, repeating myself over and over, trying to iterate inheritance until it heals. I can't flee from the contradictions I carry inside me. I've given up trying.

I hear the generator finally shut down, then watch Frank as he ambles out on to **MAIN STREET**. He stops in front of the newly fallen façade lying face down. The **SHERIFF'S OFFICE**, where the Earps stood debating before they walked down to the **O.K. CORRAL** and made history, or at least that's how *Tombstone* tells it. Fifteen seconds of male violence reenacted for the next 150 years. Frank stands there a long time. I look down to my blackbook where I've been taking notes. When my eyes rise again, he's almost disappeared back toward his trailer. I keep writing :

{ towns built for camera   built lie k **THE HISTORIC**

“ ACTION !” real or not   depending   who’s watching   who’s doing the telling }
uncle-actor hands his prop gun to Kidme   it’s so heavy kidhand can’t draw
unless there’s a hand to help him   Kidme is no artist   can’t draw **&**
why **YES** *!* of course   dress Kidme up in duds   why **YES** *!* of course
little boys love capguns &why not   they go **BLAM !** don’t they *?*   show ’em
cowboys   play em indians   raise em up to be soldiers   give ’em
a story to play   an empire to die for   look nothing about this I like   in fact
I want to hate everything about these myths   but most of all   I want to hate
how I love   the leaden embrace   of a real gun in my hand

By the time I'm driving back down the dirt track away from the set, the shadows have flipped over themselves and are stretching away back east. I feel the camera shooting me with a wide lens. I'm a small thing scurrying over the western landscape. This is a movie, or it has been, or I wish it was.

I turn south on to the pavement that takes me down to the freeway, toward home. Bumping over the train tracks, I come back into the real town of Mescal. On the way in this morning I had noticed a quiet construction site : the grasses scraped back for the metal siding of a new Dollar General. Now, passing it again, the construction crew is hard at work. They're stuccoing a rectangular wooden façade, in the process of making it look just like a real building.

GAMBELS

QUAIL FLUSH FROM MESQUITAL

FLOURISH THE GOLDEN

WINGÉD LIGHT SUNSET

LIFTING FLURRY OF

GRASSLANDS SKYWARD

GAMBLERS

FURY RUSH BLOOD

LUST MONTE FARO

ROYAL FLUSHED

TABLE FLIPPED

WINGÉD CARDS

FEATHERED AIR

ALL FALL

A YELL FULL

The Below Noon Saloon

yes I'm done with poetry   there's more money in the mirage business

I've given up on writing the book   I'm opening this here saloon instead

setting up a whole catchment for mirage   dribbling bottles full
sliding shots across the bar   to any&every page-weary wanderer
visage recursing down the neck   flooding mineshaft of throat

it's not a fancy venue   no need to get all fanced up   gunpowder the nose
just wreck in   unsuspend your disbelief   &up-spend for relief
if yer hungry I have food for thought : the finest in

rusted ephemera&seraphic ramblings   but I tire
of barking&striking all these claims   in my own haggard name   so now
when I underline my eyes   step on stage   a proscenium a lyceum a historama

I'll sing   the only news that stays news   an evanescent effusion of phraseology
no sé adonde ir from here   but I'll still take you too   past palatial ruins
to pan for future   scoop some words   spin&spin around spittoon

yes ! a **PERFORMANCE OF LANGUAGE** suitable for the **BIRD CAGE**
fortunes from the vernacular as it falls   you might think you don't understand
but o ! you do   just let the mirage wash over&through —

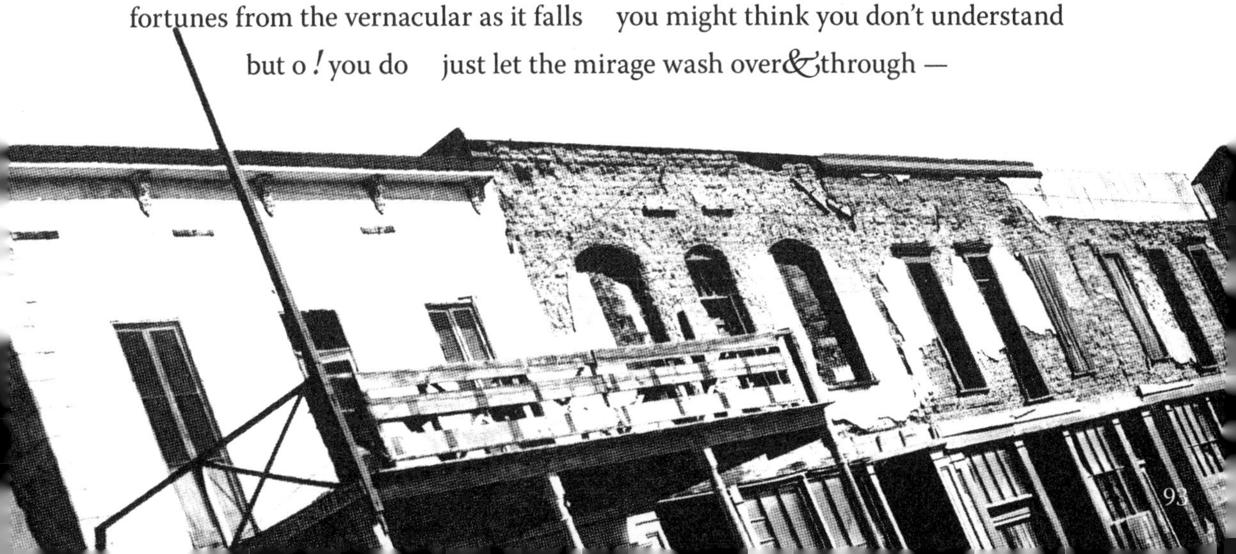

LIVE ON STAGE!

A SALOON MUSICAL

never settled for a sliver   silver-veined settlers after that
good **GOLD** ! old gods agog at the giddyup   the ungrieved verdigris
greed a veldt a vesper a ventricle   a vatic ventriloquy an inescapable soliloquy

prospecting dictionary&antiquity   a conceit an accretion amassed
aquiferous fugue artesian dirge   a PhDiddy   a doctor of alkali hauntology
foreboding   yon fiery fates   with a **YIPPY-YAY-O-CHIMERA**

a psalm a salvo a scathe a choza a choya a chacal chacalín
sí acepto mi acento de acanto de ocotillo de fronterizo mero
verso miradero   un servidor léxico un buscacantos   un encanto árido

entiendo esto de desenterrar dudas como   una encomienda
que viene encuerada   un delito doloso esto de deleitarme   una pomposidad
de polvorencía   una pena una peña   psicodinámica de cantera abandonada

la vaquería   hijinxed in jaculatorias&jacaleadas   reading the mesquite
leaves where they fall   shattered newsprint   scattered atlas
gnarled candelabra of incunabula   a bibliomancy of bosque

aquí no más leyendo lo que hay   palmas&portales   autoleyendas hechas leyes
muchos güeyes hexmeisters fight over simulacrums   o ! the scintillations salaz
heliomancers fisticuff sky scryers   o'er firmament phenomena impermanent

a prospectre spooking the past with a pickax   every hometown haunted
every utterance a code-switch   run off the rails   with a clusterfuck of dynamite
in consensus reality   an accession of heresy averred   home a phantom   uxorious lux

yes ! allusive alluvium   caught in the uvula quivering ululation   yes ! asperous tongues
sisal aloft   parryi murpheyi &all the *I* can see   all these men   all mestory mister !
another lit father fable   a memoir a minefield a montage a mutoscope a salulun

some men man &other men men   covered in quicksilver&mercurial poisoning
a group of men is called *a posse*   a group of cops *a rash*   apropos&apoplectic mob
quavering delirium tremens   desiderium desideratum   tremendo diagnosis

FREEZE ! an asphyxiating masculine alexithymia   only mezcal mumblings
&mescaline make it through   all gurgle &no guts   a life lived at ten paces
te juro que es conjuro   a talking cure   a scribbling gnosis :

I write scripts&writs&rites in **CAPS** that go **BANG-BLAM**
HANG-BLAH-BLAMMO   I'm not yelling it's all typo&too graphic
an autonovella grafted fist of gibberish   squeamish yes desierto de yeso&brillo

y eso es ser sonambulista   sorrowful in endless seek
as stopless in sibilance as rustled rattlesnakes   as a rusted
spectre-spectacle bien lost   in the snarled lexicography

dizzied with doom   wandering the micaceous wastes of whiteness
guideless pallor   osmotic paleness   getting under the skin
everywhere&nowhere as dust   a whodunnit&o ! so damn humdrum

all an ambuscade   oblivious witness   an outlaw witless   claiming
his own reward   pockets heavy with gold   on the gallows   give the self up
to escape !   reword&reclaim acidic tailings   of supremacist tall tales !

EUREKA !
I can finally see it ! Now **I KNOW** :

that **THIS** is what it means : I was born in — { doors swing open }

WHO THE HELL CARES !
{ he interrupts } **YOU AIN'T SPECIAL !**

am too ! why in fall of **'83**
Youngmother herself wrote
people think that you are unreal
but we know you are just special

O ! HOLY MOTHER MIDAS !
{ comes his retort } **EVERY TEXT**
YOU TOUCH TURNS GIDDY
O ! MY BABY CALENDAR !
O ! MY NEWSPAPER !
O ! MY MY MY !

look ! these here are my particulars
keep reading &let me finish
you might learn yourself something

O ! ALMIGHTY
MIGHTS&MAYBES
O ! INTROSPECTACLE
I TELL YOU WHAT { he says }
GET YOUR ASS OFF STAGE
LET'S STEP OUTSIDE
I'LL LEARN *YOU* HOW TO MEAN
er **HOW TO MAKE MEANING**
er **WHAT IT MEANS MAN !**

The "act Shun!"

BIRD CAGE THEATRE
1881
EAT DRINK
BIRD CAGE
OLDEST THEATRE
IN THE SOUTHWEST
EAT
HERE
EAT • DRINK
AT THE
BIRD CAGE

" ACTION ! "

why Johnny **RINGO** you look like somebody just walked over your grave

{ close-up on men's eyes }

alright lunger let's do it — I want your blood
&I want your soul &I want them
right **NOW**

I'm your huckleberry

{ close-up on men's lips }

but I ain't gonna fight you
there's no money in it

for it's a tuesday
&hardly anyone's bought tickets

because he wants to kiss Val Kilmer
TEENME will rent the VHS tape **AGAIN**

&talk about the

" ACTION ! "

talk only about the **GUNFIGHTS**
because there are words here for **GUNFIGHTS**

&fistfights &fort flights **&GUNFIGHTS** &starred
nights &mine rights **&GUNFIGHTS** &ford
lights &party sites **&GUNFIGHTS** &girl
slights &gunsights &teen rites

but not for what **TEENME** feels

for **TEENME** is thirteen
&it's a mystery what a huckleberry is

{ the sun **SET**

lingers down

his face }

TEENME thinks to himself

"

Huckleberry . . .

how could I be one   of whatever it is   too ?
because there's none here   &I don't know the words   I don't know

you philosophize Huckleberry   talk smooth   waterfall a coin
down your knuckles   twitch 'stache   you could kill   anytime
you could   teach me   to speak   but whatever
a lunger is   Huckleberry   you're dying from the unhealth   of it
&I think   this town will kill me too   but I'm being dramatic
I'm just sick   of it   &if I get arrested one more time   I'll be here forever
shoplifting   boring how the law always wins   but not against you
&besides   this is   just a movie   &not thoughts   I could really think

but say I could — *god* Johnny **RINGO** you too **O.K.**
the hellfire flashing   in those eyes   the grimace   that could be anything
your lips   off those teeth   I'm as close as I can get   to the screen

&maybe I could —

"

{ the sun **SETS**
&shoots them down with it
real   real slow }

“ ACTION ! ”

hey there **EARP**   how the hell are ya

those men you killed were my friends

well hell   maybe you shoulda stuck around
not gone off to college
&become a Flagstaff hippie

you see that *?*   says **U.S. MARSHALL**
means this is all **LEGAL**

you think a degree makes you better *?*
the hell you gonna do *?* write a poem about it *?*
lemme remind you what’s **REAL**
in **COCHISE COUNTY**
come get some sissy-boy   you pansy **FUCK**

cowboys are **DEAD** *!*
you hear me you **CUR** *?!*
EARP’s comin &hell’s comin with me *!*

{ the sun **SETS**

but make no mistake
it’s not revenge he’s after }

sometime in the **1990s** Kidsister&Kidme
on another camping trip in the Dragoons

climb up a favorite granite ridge to find a whole town has been built
in the ravine on the other side it's the **1880s**

man-sized buildings down at the mouth with men&horses all around
tiny buildings built above on the hillside like abandoned dollhouses

maybe if Kidme squints eyes into cameras
it will look less silly &yes more **REAL**

Kidme watches the shooting until sunset
waiting for a **GUNFIGHT** to break out

but there's only dialogue he can't hear
with an occasional stampede all day long the bullhorn says

"
O.K. everybody let's try that again . . .

ACTION *!* **"**

" ACTION / "

BLAM!BLAM!BLAM!BLAM!BLAM
BLAM!

Younguncle got **SHOT** !
Younguncle's body goes **STIFF** !
Younguncle's falling forward
&right off the **ROOF** !

{ a dry cloud rises
applause scatters }

Younguncle dies three times a day :

GUNFIGHTS
GUNFIGHTS
GUNFIGHTS

{ &the sun **SETS**

behind the gift shop }

Teacher's suspension protested

By CHERYLE RODRIGUEZ
Citizen Staff Writer

The suspension yesterday of an Amphitheater High School teacher who publically admitted using marijuana has triggered protests from Amphitheater students and faculty members who say the suspension was needless and unfair.

Petitions condemning the suspension of Steve Eastin, 26-year-old Varsity tennis coach and English instructor, were being circulated about the school's campus today.

Eastin said at the City Council's public hearing on marijuana laws Monday that he is a marijuana user and that possession of the drug should not be a criminal offense.

Yesterday Amphitheater School District Supt. Thomas E. Neel suspended Eastin and began an investigation into his comments at the hearing. Neel said he took the action in response to numerous public protests concerning the teacher's stand on marijuana.

Eastin's comments might constitute admission of a felony and would cost him his teaching job, Neel said.

But more than 25 Amphitheater students interviewed today by the Tucson Daily Citizen contended that Eastin is a good teacher and a good counselor, and that he should not be penalized for using marijuana in his off-duty hours.

Don Markle, faculty adviser to the school's student council, said about half the school's 70 faculty members also were opposed to the suspension.

"I can't believe he's been suspended for that reason," said Irma Bernal, 17. "He is a miraculous teacher. Students who are not even in his classes go to him for counseling . . . he always takes the time with them. And he's hardly the only teacher who smokes dope."

Chris Cunningham, 16, who is coached in tennis by Eastin,

{ Youngmother brings Kidme out to **MESCAL**
where her brother Younguncle is shooting }

" ACTION ! "

Younguncle a **REEL** cowboy !
Younguncle in a stampede !

between shots Younguncle hands Kidme his gun

it's so heavy Kidhand can't draw
or even hold the gun at arm's length
if this isn't real what is ?

Kidme gets the pretending
Younguncle &thesemen are doing :
they're cowboys even though they're not

thesemen they try it then they have to try it again

Kidme on set " **ACTION** ! " watching the stampede
set on seeing " **ACTION** ! " witness the stampede
" **ACTION** ! " in stampede
" **ACTION** ! " a stampede
" **ACTION** ! " stampeding
" **ACTION** ! " stampede
" **ACTION** ! " stampede
" **ACTION** ! " stampede
until it's boring

Tucson Daily

WEDNESDAY, APRIL 16, 1975 •

YOUNGUNCLE ALWAYS GETS IN ON THE " ACTION ! "

STEVE Eastin was a gunfighter, which was a gig one could still get in **TUCSON** in the **70s**.

Well, not Tucson proper but **OLD TUCSON**, the movie location and cowboy tourist trap out in Avra Valley. A place one could visit, until it closed in the sickly summer of **'20**. There'd been hard times for a while. The town all but burnt to the ground in **'95**. I watched the flames on the KGUN 9 News, belly down on brown carpet of the living room.

They rebuilt some of the old buildings. There was revival in the **10s** when cowboys were replaced with zombies at an annual event called **NIGHTFALL**.

Same setting, different characters. The plot? A rave-cum-zombie apocalypse. Millennials reliving the desert parties of the early **00s**. Or the **GAY 90s** even.

I wonder if a zombie gets shot like Steve : falling off a roof, rolling over an awning, biting the dust. For awhile COVID devastated even the undead, killed the myth. Then new operators came in and the zombies rode again. **NEW OLD TUCSON**.

But my Uncle Steve, he was around for the real good ol' days.

He quit his job teaching English at the University of Arizona and was in a **GUNFIGHT** the next week. He says you gotta let a thing go before

Citizen

PAGE 31

the next can come. Lived in a little place off Lester before moving out to **TRAIL'S END**. Coached tennis at Amphi High. Spoke before the Tucson City Council in support of pot. Was fired. Released a country western album. Ran for governor in **'74** and got over **300** votes. Later he moved to **LA** and went full time with the acting.

You may remember Steve from that musical classic **DIAMOND STUDS**. Or his debut in **JOE KIDD**, filmed at **OLD OLD TUCSON**. You may know him from his role as a ghost, the pitcher in **FIELD OF DREAMS**. Or the salty cop riding **CON AIR**. Or living **DAYS OF OUR LIVES**. Or from the conversation with DiCaprio in **CATCH ME IF YOU CAN**. Or the judge in **KILLERS OF THE FLOWER MOON**. That's fifty years of films.

Steve Eastin
Support pot

said, "I could care less what he does off the school grounds. He never comes to class stoned, he never blows it on campus."

Markle said his students spent the first two class periods today discussing the issue. "They (the students) feel the marijuana law is an idiotic law," Markle said.

At the conclusion of the hearing Eastin spoke, the City Council voted 5-2 to urge the State Legislature to reduce the crime of marijuana possession from a felony to a misdemeanor.

Of his public comments, Eastin said today, "I just explained at the hearing that I use marijuana and am still pretty healthy. I didn't think the criminal code reflected the true nature of the herb."

He said he would make the comments again because "there is a kind of hypocrisy in marijuana use. Many people in positions of responsibility use it."

Neel said he and the school district's attorney would conduct the investigation and report their findings to the school board.

Eastin is receiving full pay during his suspension and the investigation.

When I was a kid, he'd appear out of nowhere, hawking insurance or stretching a buck for El Campo Tires during commercial breaks. He really let his charisma carry him. Synchronicity. Talent too.

Oldunclealways talked about writing down the stories I've heard a million times. Then he finally did, called his book *Born in a Fatal Car Crash : . . . And Other Dramatic Entrances.* Olduncle says my book made him do it. Tells me he left out a lot of stuff that was too hurtful or too close to publish.

The family has always made a big deal of our similarities. Brown eyes and cheek bones, the lone boychild surrounded by sisters and girlcousins. Growing up, my extended family was fifteen people. Six grandkids, and I was the only boy. I've always been more myself around women, and I was raised by powerful women who never took shit from anybody : Evelyn, Mary, Deedee, Judy, Cass, Lanee, Shayne, Ali, Danica.

But holidays I'd find myself sitting in while my two uncles needled each other over politics. And I still do. This also feels like home, being between an actor and a lawyer. Remembering and misremembering, debating how the hell it came to this.

In a different draft of the script, I moved to **LA** and became an actor. I got ears-deep into cocaine. Started a band, rode a motorcycle, went to law school, leather jacket, the whole bit.

Robbed enough stages that I could cash out and disappear on to a ranch down on the San Pedro.

But instead I'm here in my version of Tucson, making this life. Raising two kids, two girls, learning as I go. Cultivating this patch of land, growing pot that's finally legal. Teaching English at the university, getting laid off, waking before dawn to write **GUNFIGHTS**, falling over and over and over.

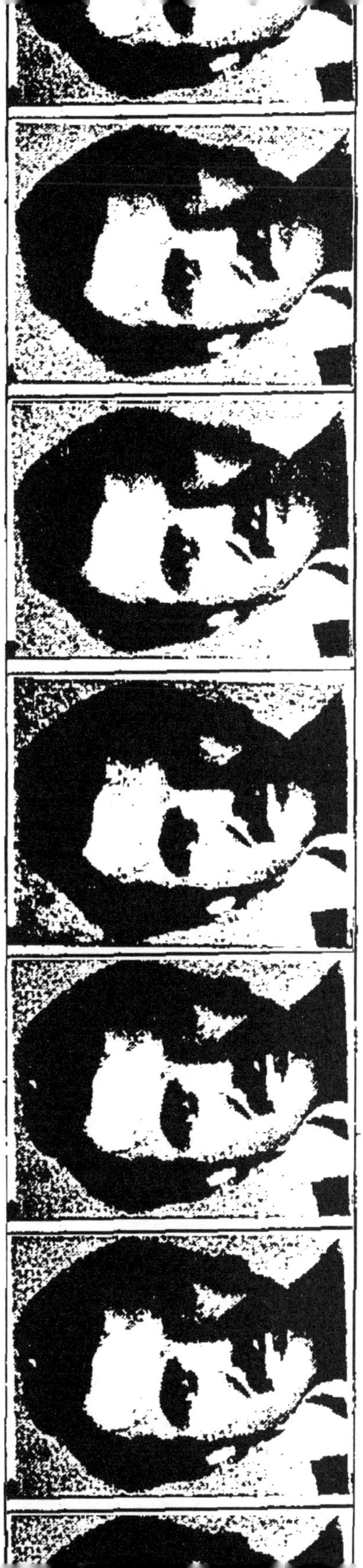

{ Kidme comes back to Tombstone
sticks kidfinger in a **REAL** bullethole
thumb&forefinger a sixshooter twice }

" STICKEMUP EVERYBODY " this is a childhood
a boy is being raised here a storybook being written

in

GUNSCRIPT
GUNSCRIPT
GUNSCRIPT

with

cowboys&indians *!*
cops&robbers *!*
migrants&migra *!*
EARPs&CLANTONs *!*
white ranchers&buffalo soldiers *!*

"
O.K. pretend this is my horse &I'm so fast
O.K. pretend I'm a robber &I steal the stagecoach
O.K. pretend I'm in court &I defend myself
&I get acquitted &pretend &pretend it's all just

ACTION *!* "

EXT. - ALLEN STREET - HIGHNOON

{ two figures step in slow circles&circles
hands hover holsters   the silence brittle as pane }

TEENME&KIDME
lock squint-eyes —
gonna **GUNFIGHT** !

meanwhile — Grownme   over here   in the shadows this whole time
a gun in each hand   ready   to win it all
how real gunfights are always won   right in the back

but then I waver   still reckoning
how to write   a moment of a truth
how to draw something   other than a gun

for in the end
there's no duel ex machina

it won't be a gunfight
that ends all gunfights

{ the sun sets
in the background
cutting a silhouette
in retrospection }

{ the sunsets
a kerosene lamp tossed
into Bird Cage curtains }

{ the sun set :
where the movie version
of the sun was filmed in **'93** }

{ the sun sets
a lump in a
thirsty throat }

{ the sun sets
a coin rolling into slot
mechanical fortune-teller cowboy }

{ the sun sets
&gets the drop
on the whole town }

{ the sun sets
neon punctuation a saloon
he's a sign a wet paperback dried
face unfurling o my god
a prayer heaved o sky pilot }

EXT. - COCHISE COUNTY - SUNSET

The Huachuca Mountains a jagged silhouette.

Slow flyover, tight shot from above.
Red dirt, clumps of pale grass, dark mesquite.
A bolting of rabbits. A scramble of quail.
A diamondback rattlesnake threads the foliage.

Quickening, the camera pans up, landscape blurring into
rolling grassland, broken only by the horizon.

A **HOUSE** comes into view, dark pink stucco, large windows
reflect sky. Back porch, a glass-top patio table
covered in beer bottles. Men sit. Camera stops. Tight shot.

The younger of the two, balding, gesticulates.
The remains of a marijuana cigarette smolder between his fingers.
The older man, gray haired, takes a drink.

GROWNSON: . . . so he's penniless, nearing the end of his life and needs to come up with some money to leave for his young wife — so he decides to sell his story, the story of Tombstone.

OLDDAD: Huh, so what year is this?

GROWNSON: 20s. Forty-some years after the whole thing. And also he's pissed — these articles are being written that vilify him, public opinion has it that he and his brothers were the bad guys. He's famously a man of few words, right, but he gets this young guy to take down his account. Problem is, this guy John Flood isn't a writer. He's a mining engineer, and the writing just sucks. Nobody will publish it. Then this novelist named Burns steals the story and writes *Tombstone: An Iliad of the Southwest,* the book that sets it all up.

GROWNSON: Earp ends up working as a consultant on westerns, which are just getting started. I didn't realize that — Hollywood started with westerns! Well, westerns and *The Birth of a Nation.* But here was Earp, still alive and the mythologizing was already underway, turning the bad guys into the good guys. I thought there was a lag, some gap between when all the shit happened and when they started writing it.

GROWNSON: And in the movie *Tombstone* from **'93** — remember how many times I watched that in high school?! — the last scene is Earp's funeral, there's this voice-over saying the pallbearers included early western star Tom Mix. It ends with the line — right from Jarre's screenplay — it ends "Tom Mix wept." What a strange ending! Why do we care?! The movie was so desperate to place itself in the lineage. It's so meta! It even starts with bogus documentary footage, making it look like there were movie cameras in Tombstone in the **80s**, like the movie is loyal to some historical document. *But the actors are in the footage! Val Fuckin Kilmer!* It's all been recursive since forever, iteration after iteration inverting, folding in on themselves, the story more real than its subject. A fractal. And that's a fact.

GROWNSON: So you know how by the **20s** the mining boom busted, and the county seat was moved from Tombstone to Bisbee, and there was nothing left but a ghost town in the making. Well, that's when they started the gunfight reenactments! In **'29**, the year Earp died! It's practically concurrent nostalgia, which is so American and serves a specific purpose. They say in real life Earp's last words were "**SUPPOSE, SUPPOSE**." So if there was no real interlude between the events and the story-making, you gotta wonder if the story was there first.

OLDDAD: Well, I'm pretty sure I'm the one who told you about most of this stuff. But I'm not following you with the story thing. How do you mean?

GROWNSON: *Story* sent Schieffelin into the Tombstone Hills in the first place! The Seven Cities of Gold was a trope even before the Spanish came to Las Américas. They inscribed this place with the stories they carried, like Kino planting wheat around his missions. The New World was incomprehensible, so they defaulted to what they knew. Catholicism, conquista, Cíbola, treasure. Coronado, de Niza. Everything they had been steeped in for the previous eight hundred years while fighting the Moors, the original darker-skinned "savages" in their minds. Acequias, haboobs, javelinas. *Alcohol, jinete, ojalá, alfalfa.* All words from Arabic. They absorbed the language, then turned *this* desert into *that* desert, naming as they went. I mean, I've been trying to write this for years!

OLDDAD: But what does that have to do with Tombstone?

GROWNSON: It's all the same thing! Sure, Kino, Schieffelin, and Jarre were a couple centuries apart, but they were actors in the same play. In the **80s** Tombstone boomed to be the biggest town between St. Louis and San Francisco based on *stories* of silver, not silver itself. Like somebody said, "There might be silver in the hills and blood on the streets, but there was gold in the print shops." Even the name came from a prediction, a story-to-be, what they told Schieffelin at Fort Huachuca before he set out to prospect : "All you'll find out in those hills is your tombstone," because of the Apaches. What I'm saying is, during the quote unquote *real* events, the people, the Earps, the Clantons, the nobodies, were all playing characters. They all came to reinvent themselves and strike it rich.

OLDDAD: Just like the old fogies that retire to Tombstone to play cowboys, walking around and posing for pictures.

GROWNSON: *Exactly, Dad!* And get this, during the filming of *Tombstone,* a whole tent city sprung up near the Mescal set. Kevin Cost — I mean Kurt Russell — called all these guys "the buckaroos." They came from all over to be extras in the movie! And they let them! Just said that they wouldn't be paid and had to look the part. So they lived in their tents and RVs, cooked out there, stayed in costume, real mustaches. The whole thing was cosplay. Method acting. The hordes of treasure seekers descended on Mescal during the filming just like they did on Tombstone a century prior. Not silver ore but silver screen, the allure still the same. A lucky strike, fifteen seconds of fame. And it worked out for some of them : they got their names in the credits.

EARP • CLANTON
HUCKLEBERRY • RINGO

KIDDAD • YOUNGFATHER
OLDFATHER • OLDDAD
YOUNGMOTHER • YOUNGMOM

BABYME • TODDLERME
KIDME • TEENME
GROWNME • GROWNSON • OLDME

YOUNGUNCLE • OLDUNCLE
KIDSISTER • TODDLERKIDS

TEXAS JACK VERMILION
TURKEY CREEK JACK JOHNSON
EL CHERO MÍSTICO y QUERIDO

CURLY BILL • MCLAURY
ALLIE EARP • MR. FABIAN
MILT JOYCE • PONY DIEHL
SHERIFF SLAUGHTER • GEN. CROOK
NINO COCHISE • C.S. FLY

1ST GAMBLER • 1ST COWBOY POET
AUDIENCE MEMBER • GANG BOSS
ARMY RECRUITER • HIGH SCHOOLER
BUFFALO SOLDIER • BORDER PATROL
AGGRIEVED RANCHER • DEFENDANT

CAMERA MAN • TUCSON CASTING
HEAD BUCKAROO WRANGLER
GUNSCRIPT SUPERVISOR
HAIR&MAKEUP EXPLORER
SIERRA VISTA WEED DEALER
BISBEE GRAFFITI IDOL CRUSH
SPECIAL AFFECTS

BABOCOMARI RANCH
LUCKY CUSS MINING CO.
OLD TUCSON STUDIOS - MESCAL
CRYSTAL ICE OF ARIZONA

SCENES DEPICTING MALE VIOLENCE
WERE SIMULATED

MCMLXXXIII

FILMED IN PANAVISION®

ORIGINAL SOUNDTRACK AVAILABLE ON INTRADA

SPECTRAL RECORDING DOLBY STEREO SR™

NO. 32851

THIS PICTURE MADE UNDER THE JURISDICTION OF

COME SEE a man
build a campfire   from a red light bulb
&ribbon ripped cellophane

YES a man
can span several sites
making **MUSEUMS** of each
first **TOMBSTONE**   then **FORT HUACHUCA**
a former courthouse   a former theater
two sides of the same river valley
the defense   the performance
of **HISTORY**

the **APACHE SCOUTS**
the **BUFFALO SOLDIERS**
narrated for tourists   again&again

here **YOU** can
meet the past
FACE-TO-FACE
feel like you're there
as if   you never left

The COURTHOUSE MUSEUM

EXHIBIT

" look Logan

for the next exhibit
I'm building a campout scene
I have the mannequins ready

but needed these —
we found a lady out of state
who makes them

{ Youngfather opens
cake boxes of decapitations

finely sculpted faces
Black&Apache&white

glass marble eyes
stare into Kidme a terror }

don't they look

real ? "

EXHIBIT

" look Logan

you know he died violently
because this big jagged hole
right here in the back

— see ?

{ Youngfather holds the human skull
places it back on the shelf   metal government gray

opens another archive
from the drawer pulls out a paper

with an original signature
of **ABRAHAM LINCOLN** }

now look

at this . . . "

EXHIBIT

history is an old theater
turned museum turned
replica desert evening
where Kidme steps
on a hidden switch
&a coyote calls from a tape loop

history auto-rewinds unseen
beneath a fiberglass boulder

backstage in the archive
history is just what dad did
taught himself to build exhibits
how to spell letter-by-letter
the text given to him

TAXONOMYTAXIDERMY
hawk skunk rattlesnake den
who won what war when

history is not what happened
but how it is told
on Take Your Son to Work Day

EXHIBIT

while **TOMBSTONE** had
a reputation for lawlessness
the town of **CHARLESTON**
eight miles away on the San Pedro
was even more rowdy

built in the **70s** to give workers from
MILLVILLE a place to live&drink

mercury poisoned as they were
pain flooded prone
to fits of rage
with money to blow

once the Tombstone mines
hit water the mill of Millville
was taken down &reconstructed
in Tombstone &there was
no more meaning for Charleston

later **U.S. ARMY** used the ghost
town to train Black infantrymen for
WORLD WAR II
history an adobe maze
toward future wars

don't visit the ruins today
potentially hazardous munitions
could still be present

h i s t o r y
an unclaimed bomb

EXHIBIT

back in **’89 U.S. ARMY** soldiers were escorting wagons full of coins to Fort Thomas

when in a gorge they were **AMBUSHED** *!* in a flood of lead &**GUNMEN** got the gold

gunmen so bold they left their white faces uncovered &rode right back to their own ranches with the loot of **$ 9 6 0 , 5 0 0**

later in **FEDERAL COURT** every **BUFFALO SOLDIER** — still recovering from wounds &having been decorated for bravery — testified against them

then watched the ranchers be **A C Q U I T T E D** by a jury of their peers

afterward even the judge commented on the obvious racial animus { against Black soldiers some born into enslavement now free &working for the feds in Arizona

a territory that had aspired to slave state but was too late postbellum }

one assailant named **WT** was later elected **SPEAKER** of the **TERRITORIAL HOUSE OF REPRESENTATIVES** &often boasted of the robbery telling it thus :

“ I neither confirm nor deny any involvement for to confirm would be to admit my **GUILT** but to deny would surely spoil a **GOOD STORY** ”

EXHIBIT

this dry lush land cared for
over millennia of lifetimes
by the O'odham&ancestors
grass grown tall in story&culture

cattle arrived then the train
cowboys didn't own the cows
they spent their lives working

cattle the technology
by which this land's wide richness
was ingested extracted into
private profit for stockholders

grasslands turned meat shipped
east from railhead at Benson
it's not the cow's fault

land turned hardscrabble shale
scrub creosote ocotillo gray
land turned range
ground into hamburger
a steak out still bleeding
cattle cattle cattle cattle cattle cattle

this isn't blaming
this is telling what happened
to who where when

somebody ate a burger in **1883**

this land became some body
energy for factory work
until they died
&this land was buried in a coffin
{ if one could be afforded }

but don't worry
this was a long time ago

&nothing stays dead long

so now this land is everywhere
again in my dusty inhale

now exhaled in the stories I tell
the work I do
or choose not to

EXHIBIT

in the **90s** my high school
history teacher { the one who
licked his lips &gave girls A's }

he said

“ **ILLEGALS**
are invading Cochise County

&that's what's wrong
with **AMERICA** !
they're damn thieves ”

then history was canceled

but just for a day
so we could go to the library
to hear a special guest

a **REAL** cowboy
to inspire us to write
our own { **COWBOY** } **POETRY**

the first poet I'd ever met
sepia skinned &in costume

he said

“ don't change with the times
for only sand's a true sonnet

real poetry rhymes
this land with us on it ”

EXHIBIT

back before Kidme there was Younguncle
    riding high after a speaking role
    in *Joe Kidd*   Old Tucson Studios
&before him was Tom Mix
    &other white actors squinting
    in westerns

but before them were Mexican vaqueros
    working stock owned by capitalists
    in Tucsón   state of Sonora
&before them were poor españoles
    herding cattle for conquistadores
    on O'odham lands   called Nueva España
&before them were peasants
    raising cowherds for Catholic kings
    in Extremadura   old España
&before them were Moors
    ruling Iberia for eight centuries
    on horseback   Black African

COWBOYS

another American culture with African roots
that Kidme was never told about

EXHIBIT

EARP killed **CLANTON**
HUCKLEBERRY killed **RINGO**
train killed wagon
interstate killed train
Oregon Trail killed class time
settler killed the buffalo
typhoid killed the settler
boys killed their tears
cowboys killed poetry
army recruiters killed time
Circle K killed Little General
Pelon Pelo Rico killed tongue
torta killed sandwich
algorithm killed newspaper
moving picture killed troupe
VHS killed Betamax
O.K. sure TV killed radio star
cloud killed physical
LED stage killed location shoot
greed killed Hollywood
selfie killed C. S. Fly
trappers killed beaver
earthquake killed Charleston
head cut killed ciénaga
pump killed cottonwood
border wall killed jaguar
subdivision killed foothills
influencers killed barrio
poker killed faro
profit margin killed voting booth
missile manufacturer killed aquifer
bomb factory workers killed kids
city fathers killed Apache babies
Tucson police killed Carlos
Border Patrol killed José Elena
minutemen killed Brisenia
ICE agents killed family
Bisbee killed Tombstone
Airbnb killed Bisbee
reenactment killed history
&so who kills who next *?*

EXHIBIT

AMERICAN WEST®
FOR AGES OVER 8 NO. 7004
ROLL CAPS
6 BOXES • 1500 SHOTS
ESQUIRE/NICHOLS®
AMSTERDAM, NY 12010 MADE IN CANADA
AMERICAN WEST by esquire®
CAPS
FOR REPEATING PISTOLS
5 ROLLS 250 SHOTS

EXHIBIT

Marjorie Reed

GETTING HERE

ride   down the freeway
        off the I-10
        out **MESCAL ROAD**
past the bar&grill
past the single-wides
        roses&nopales&flagpoles
until you hit the train tracks
        the land-grab sutures
until the pavement ends
        the frontier cattle guarded
until the dirt narrows
past the dry flurry
        of **PRIVATE**
        PROPERTY signs
        windblown&bulletholed
until the barbed wire goes limp
until the dirt corrugates
until the washboard becomes
        MAIN STREET
        of a movie set
until the boomtown becomes
        a twopenny ghost town
you keep going
until **MAIN STREET** becomes
        a two track
until the two track becomes
        a game trail
until the game trail becomes
        a trace
until the trace becomes bootprints
until your boots imprint through
        the warped doorframe of
        a roofless miner's shack
until you run out the back
        &right down
        the bottomless mineshaft
you just keep going   until you see

EXHIBIT

EXHIBIT

EXHIBIT

EXHIBIT

what we in our ignorance
believe to be impossible.
I am writing you in the hopes
to satisfy a fear
brought up on the West as
much as you were.

EXHIBIT

LOS MUERTOS ~~NO~~ HABLAN
1880'S OR 1980'S GHOST STORY
"As a ghost, he didn't scare me,
APPROX. 90 MINS. / CAT. NO. 31061
resident of the ghost town,
but then, when he turned into a bat
that bothered me," the woman said.

EXHIBIT

PAINTED
Huachuca
as
hiding
he faced
the crowd
episodic
Landscape
COCHISE CO. ARIZONA TER.
perception of
advertised as "a true
self-proclaimed
stimuli

Inner theatrical sense of self
Outer theatrical sense of self
14
12
11
10
4
Historama
5
Embodiment
FOR THE ENTIRE FAMILY
the role
9
Logan
atone
Phillips
VISION
Wednesdays, Thursdays & Fridays at 7 P.M.
Saturdays at 6 & 9 P.M. • Sundays at 4 & 7 P.M.
GESTALT
Bang
I still see light. Hear
I feel needed here.
closure
proximity
continuation
figure and ground
(tree within the letter "A")
WE
BC
ME
VE
DH
FM
TM
Bang!
FINAL 2 WEEKS!
BIRD CAGE THEATRE
code reflected the true nature
there is a kind of hypocrisy
90s 10 20 30 FT

{ I was born in a town out in the riddle of know-where   I'm from
a series of scenes   I flick the photo album forward&back so fast
many still photographs taken together give the illusion of movement }

BABYME's Tombstone neighbors : western painter Marjorie Reed
who Youngdad begs for another commission   &The World's Largest
Rose Tree   still selling tickets   the only survivor of the 1880s
held up by a structure built in the 1930s   metal sagging

KIDME holds his face to the B&W 8.5 x 11" glossy historic official reprint
a 1886 photograph by C. S. Fly   that Youngdad brings home from work
warriors   an Apache baby   meeting Kidme's eyes   &he can tell you
their names :   *Perico Geronimo Naiche Tsisnah*

KIDME looks out his bedroom window   toward the pale blue Whetstones
stuck on the glass : a museum gift   a clear decal enlarged to 2'   art from 1888
so for his eyes to reach the horizon   Kidme has to see through a gunfight

TEENME slices a nickel in half   with industrial paper cutter   ruins the blade
with Xavi&David   working in the high school printshop   learning layout
&West Coast rap : *2001* Kurupt&Xzibit   What U See Is What U Get   but
no one wants the bad kids' two cents   just the behavior referrals they print

TEENME trickles one graffiti GIF at a time   down the dial-up 14.4 kbps
modem dialing long distance to Tucson   escapes to GeoCities on Netscape
posts first poems on Everything2   AOL CD-ROM a scattered mirror
VHS shattered by car tire   Yaqui Street   magnetic tape glittering mesquite

GROWNME opens a box of memorabilia saved by Youngmom   unfolds
The Tombstone Epitaph LOCAL EDITION VOL. CIII. NO. 26 APRIL 22 TO MAY 6
1983   finds his **BIRTH**   wonders what to do with the news   begins writing
new stories under the old headlines   wanders down into whispered memory

TEENME headbangs his grown-out hair   at a Blackfire show in Flagstaff
sees Kidme's favorite C. S. Fly Apache photo on a T-shirt   with the words
Fighting Terrorism Since 1492   meets Klee Benally   his father&family
ditches Journalism 101   to hear Winona LaDuke give a teach-in on empire
September 23, 2001   fills up his blackbook   entire pages of questions

TEENME becomes a twenty-something   &organizes a solidarity caravan from
Flagstaff back to Cochise County   where the 2006 publisher of the *Epitaph*
rallies anti-immigrant vigilantes   just as Clum had done against the Chinese
we yell poems at the Naco border   at the end of the wall   we play volleyball

KIDME pedals his bike on a candy run to Little General   the gas station
on the far side of Pueblo del Sol II   neighborhood's street names :   Indigenous
peoples who don't live there   take Cherokee to Kiowa   ride Sioux to Hwy. 92

KIDME becomes a middle schooler &curses cursive   takes up Dad's hand
writing each letter in caps   { &so now I still write slow slow   flipping back
through my blackbook   to find my poems written   in Dad's handwriting }

BABYME becomes a kindergartner   at Huachuca Mountain Elementary
learns to read   using newspaper columns   underlining with NO. 2 pencil
the words he recognizes :   *but to the with   and a who*

Earp Clanton Huckleberry Heath thesemen they all died with nothing
except their names in the *Epitaph* after lifetimes of Contention&Lucky Cuss
but don't worry I've stopped looking to dead gunfighters for life advice
&I don't need an Epistaffer to tell me Tombstone a town I don't remember

except when we laugh over stories : sure Mom&Dad remember Flowers
remember the phone ringing at midnight : bats in the Courthouse again
remember the wheelbarrows of dirt making of the mudhouse a place to live

remember the gulch out back filled with last century's ladles&spoons
remember Marjorie in her shack painting Dad's wedding present to Mom :
Tim & Judy's Tombstone Marjorie filling an old mineshaft with car bodies

Mom teaching in Sierra Vista driving back&forth on the unfenced range
of Charleston Road the time a cow almost got us killed on a blind curve
the car spinning spinning spinning a whole circle &Babyme giggling

the time Mom looked out the kitchen window to see Toddlerme in a diaper
sitting on a crater covered in red ants she sprinted to door as babyscreams
pierced walls — *&I've never been the same since* I wisecrack the earth inside me

when I ask Mom if she remembers gunfighters on my bedroom window
she says *no* *it wasn't gunfighters* *I never would've allowed that*
but when I find the grainy photo I took in '95 squinting they're still gunning

but look this history isn't a blame we barely remember
the people we were then &they both did so good
better than was done to them

Mom remembers staring in love   falling into my eyes   but I don't — I know
their love as   sun rays through oak leaves   sparkle of water down steps
always the deep of me   in this life together   no matter the part I'm playing

Dad has always
said   *I love you son*
meaning it   more than anything

I believe him
I always have

&now here I am   a youngfather

sitting on the earth in the backyard   with these twin toddlerkids
who grab at the wet dirt   pack it into red plastic molds   building mudcastles
that harden to adobe   in tender Tucson sun   in Barrio Viejo behind

a mudhouse of my own   a garden I've planted with birds-of-paradise
for these kids growing wild   kids who call the ocotillos *uncletíos*
kids who have never seen a gunfight   who don't even know the word for *gun*

American kids   who hear   twenty gunshots down the street
&look up excited saying   *firewords dada firewords !*
I will tell my children the truth   a little at a time

Esme scribbles to make whole books   before she can even form letters
Isadora draws &cuts out   a hundred hearts   each with a set of eyes
these kids   they help me to see   maybe history is

what I do with it   what I'm willing to do   to heal
the wounds I didn't inflict   to see this land not for the dead
their small stone monuments   inscriptions&newsprint

but earth as living   mud squishing   between their tiny fingers
&maybe it means   we're here to help this desert   survive us
so I will teach my children   to love the people   to love this land

once the kids learn to walk
we drive the long dirt road
threading out to the Dragoons

we lay the blanket under an oak

I teach them how to climb up the rocks

this quiet contains everything

{ the sun sets

running from
the corners
of my eyes

as I see them
hear it }

PINKGOLD GRANITE WARM WITH WINTER SUN

KIDS + I CLIMB AMIDST HOME-

SIZED BOULDERS

BENEATH ONE A CAVERN

A MOUTH LOW NARROW PROPORTIONS OF A CHILD

OF A MAN PROSTRATE ON EARTH

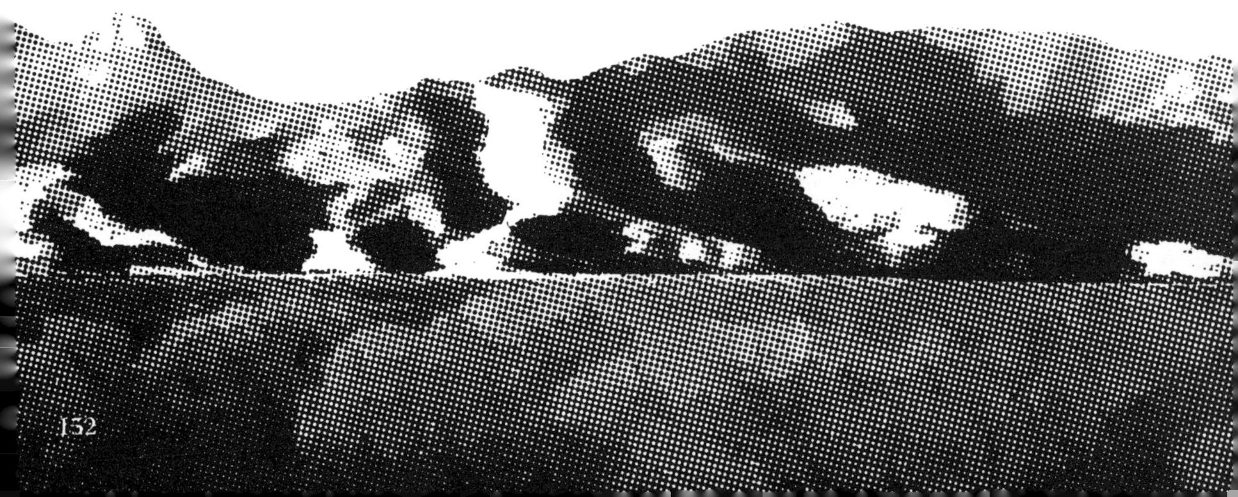

AMID INK DARK AT FAR BACK

WE SEE SOMETHING

CATCHING SUNSET SHIMMERING

A GLIMMER A GLIMPSE

NOTES

2 **Map.** "San Pedro Valley," from *Ghost Town Trails,* website now defunct.

4 **"Births."** *The Tombstone Epitaph Local Edition,* April 22 to May 6, 1983. Author's collection.

6 **Photograph.** Russell Lee, "Sign at the Outskirts of Tombstone, Arizona," 1940. Library of Congress.

7 **Photograph** by author. "Benson to St. David to Tombstone," 2019.

8 **John Heath** (also spelled "Heith"). This is an infamous Cochise County story of vigilante justice by a "Bisbee mob," told in a display at Tombstone Courthouse State Park and captured in a photo by C. S. Fly. **Boothill Graveyard** was one of Tombstone's earliest tourist attractions.

9 **Advertisements.** *The Tombstone Epitaph Local Edition,* April 22 to May 6, 1983.

10 **". . . older graveyard underneath the Dollar Tree."** Bruce Burnett, "Boothill Graveyard . . . the Most Asked Questions Answered!" *Tombstone Times,* January 2025. **William S. Oury,** former Texas Ranger, first appointed mayor of Tucson in 1864, was a lead participant in the Camp Grant Massacre of Apache people in 1871 and the first president of the Arizona Pioneers' Historical Society. **John Brackett "Pie" Allen** was Arizona's first surveyor general in 1880. **Major General John C. Frémont** led several massacres of Indigenous peoples in California, 1845–1846.

11 **Photograph** by author. "Views of Brunckow," 2021.

12 **Advertisements** and various articles by *Epitaph* staff. *The Tombstone Epitaph Local Edition,* Vol. CIII, 1982–1983, author's personal collection and University of Arizona Libraries, Special Collections. **"Stuntman switch . . ."** Edwin S. Finkelstein, *Tucson Daily Citizen,* July 20, 1972, p. 22.

13 **Photograph.** Judy Phillips, "Tim and Logan at Tumacacori," 1983. **"Collectors Items,"** *The Tombstone Epitaph National Edition,* 1983, University of Arizona Libraries, Special Collections.

14 **Photograph.** Alford E. Turner, "Chandler Milk Ranch," from *The Earps Talk* (Creative Publishing Company: Early West Series, 1980), p. 16.

16 **"The declaration . . ."** Sarah Churchwell, "Can American Democracy Survive Donald Trump?" *The Guardian,* Guardian News and Media, November 21, 2020. **Untitled illustration.** Turner, *The Earps Talk,* p. 53B.

18 **"Historic . . ." and "Letter."** *The Tombstone Epitaph Local Edition,* December 17, 1982, University of Arizona Libraries, Special Collections. **Photograph.** Judy Phillips, "Tim and Logan in the Tombstone House," 1983. **"Camping,"** poem by author, 1992. **Advertisements.** *Tucson Daily Citizen,* April 14, 1976, p. 27.

19 **Photograph.** Tim Phillips, "Logan on a Bike Ride in the Patagonias," 1984.

24 **Digital still** from 8-mm film. Tim Phillips, "Logan Swinging in Tombstone," 1984.

25 **Digital still** from 8-mm film. Tim Phillips, "Logan Rides Old Charleston Road with Cousins Lanee & Cass," 1984.

26 **Photograph** by author. "Huachuca Mountains from Ruins of Millville," 2021.

29 **Photograph.** Dorothea Lange, "Sign entering Tombstone, Arizona," 1937. Farm Security Administration - Office of War Information Photograph Collection, Library of Congress.

30 **"Here lies Lester Moore . . . ,"** a famous epitaph at Boothill Graveyard, is given a cameo in the movie *Tombstone* (1993). **Photograph** by author. "Early Morning in Mescal," 2020.

33 **Definitions** here are from Robert N. Smead, *Vocabulario Vaquero / Cowboy Talk: A Dictionary of Spanish Terms from the American West* (University of Oklahoma Press, 2004).

34 **Inspired by text** on a historical display at the Pima County Courthouse, 2019.

38 **Photograph.** Russell Lee, "Abandoned building with characteristic false front in Tombstone, Arizona," 1940. Library of Congress.

40 **Photograph.** Steven Graubart, "Reminiscing at the Old Gleeson Bar," *The Tombstone Epitaph Local Edition,* April 22 to May 6, 1983.

42 **"The first act of violence . . ."** bell hooks, *The Will to Change: Men, Masculinity, and Love* (Washington Square Press, 2004).

46 **"Give up your arms . . ."** is paraphrased from Virgil Earp's testimony at an inquest into the O.K. Corral shootout, found in Turner, *The Earps Talk.* Though legally cleared of any wrongdoing, the epitaph on the supposed grave site of the men killed reads, "Murdered on the streets of Tombstone." **"A sanguinary affray"** is from Walter Noble Burns's novel *Tombstone: An Iliad of the Southwest*, 1927.

47 **Photograph** by author. "Shadow Meets Mescal," 2020. **Photograph** by C. S. Fly, "After the fire," 1882.

51 **"Rehearsal."** *The Tombstone Epitaph Local Edition,* October 8, 1982. **"'Shatterhand' Rides Again . . ."** *Tucson Daily Citizen,* September 22, 1971, p. 14. **"Helldorado."** *The Tombstone Epitaph Local Edition,* September 26, 1980. Author's collection. **"Nino Cochise In . . ."** *The Tombstone Epitaph Local Edition,* April 22 to May 6, 1983. While many, many newspaper reporters published his claims between 1954 and 1985, he is best closely examined—and disputed—by Mary Ann Aposhian in "Will the Real Nino Cochise Please Stand?" *Tucson* magazine 3, no. 10 (October 1977). I'm grateful to the work of Angela Aleiss in *Hollywood's Native Americans: Stories of Identity and Resistance* (Bloomsbury Publishing, 2022) for leading me to Aposhian. **"A local high school teacher . . ."** *The Yuma Daily Sun,* May 31, 1974, p. 2.

52 **Photograph.** Turner, "Ruins of the Clanton Ranch House Located on the San Pedro River," *The Earps Talk*, p. 56. **"An aria at this crisis . . ."** is from Burns, *Tombstone.*

54 **Photograph** by author. "Sheriff's Office Face Down in the Dust," 2020. An auxiliary movie location long owned by Old Tucson Studios, Mescal is where *Tombstone* was filmed in 1993. The set was in disrepair and scheduled for demolition before being bought by a group of locals in 2021, when renovations were begun. **Kidme photos** by Tim and Judy Phillips.

56 **Photograph** by author. "Dragoons from the Other Cemetery," 2025.

58 **Photograph.** Doug Clay, published in Ben T. Traywick, *Wyatt Earp's Thirteen Dead Men* (Red Marie's Bookstore, 1998).

59 **"A sky dripping . . ."** is from a deleted scene in the *Tombstone* original screenplay, written by Kevin Jarre, 1993.

64 **Advertisements.** *Tucson Daily Citizen,* April 16, 1975; July 16, 1975; August 8, 1975; April 14, 21, 23, 1976; May 12, 1976.

65 **"Guard derails . . ."** *The Tucson Citizen,* January 30, 1976. **"Legalize pot" and "Pondering proverbs."** *The Tucson Citizen,* May 5, 1975. **"Natas: The Reflection."** VHS tape back cover. The movie, filmed at Mescal and the offices of the *Arizona Daily Star,* occasionally surfaces on YouTube if you really want to see it. **"Cochise County."** Kearney Egerton, "The Fascinating Fourteen Arizona Counties," *The Arizona Republic,* reprinted with permission by The Branding Iron Press, 1977. Bill Phillips (author's grandfather) collection. **". . . invention of the halftone process . . ."** Thomas Vaughan, *Journal of Arizona History* 30, no. 3 (Autumn 1989): 303–318.

66 **Digital still.** *Tombstone,* directed by George P. Cosmatos. Hollywood Pictures, 1993. This thunderstorm scene shows the Mescal set.

67 **Photographs** throughout this section are by the author. Mescal, Arizona, 2020.

92 **Photograph.** Historic American Buildings Survey. "Old City Hall, Fremont Street, Tombstone, Cochise County, AZ," 1937. Library of Congress.

97 **Photograph.** Russell Lee, "Bird Cage Theater, scene of riotous entertainment during the mining boom days. Tombstone, Arizona," 1940. Library of Congress.

98 **Poems** throughout this section sample language from Jarre's screenplay *Tombstone.*

104 **Advertisements.** *Tucson Daily Citizen,* August 8, 1975; April 14, 1976. **"Teacher's suspension . . ."** *Tucson Daily Citizen,* April 16, 1975. **Digital stills** of Steve Eastin in *Joe Kidd,* directed by John Sturges. The Malpaso Company, 1972.

107 **Advertisements.** *Tucson Daily Citizen,* May 12, 1976, p. 27.

108 **"Teacher's Suspension Protested."** *Tucson Daily Citizen,* April 16, 1975, p. 31. **Advertisement.** "Steve as the El Campo Tires Buckstretcher." *Tucson Daily Citizen,* June 13, 1975, p. 15.

109 **Headshots** of Steve Eastin from advertisements in the *Tucson Daily Citizen,* various issues. 1976.

110 **Digital stills** of Steve Eastin in *Joe Kidd.*

112 **Photograph.** Judy Phillips, "Logan and Steve on Location in Mescal," ca. 1989.

119 **"There might be silver . . ."** Douglas D. Martin, *Tombstone's Epitaph* (University of New Mexico Press, 1951).

121 **Enlargement** from photograph by author, "Bedroom Window," ca. 1995. A rendering by Tim Phillips of Frederic Remington's 1888 engraving, "A Fight in the Street."

123 **Photograph.** Russell Lee, "Abandoned courthouse. Tombstone, Arizona," 1940. Library of Congress.

126 **The Fort Huachuca Historical Museum's Annex** was originally a theater, built mostly with troop labor in 1934. Beginning in the late 1980s, the Annex centered a life-sized diorama of cavalry soldiers from Fort Huachuca (founded in 1877) camping while on patrol against "Apache depredations." The perimeter of the space had other exhibits, each housed in the false front of a replica 1880s building. All of this was largely designed and built by Tim Phillips. In 2015, years after Tim's retirement, the building was repurposed to house only a history of military Unmanned Aerial Vehicles (drones), which were tested first at Fort Huachuca in the 1950s. "Command, Control, Communications, Computers, Intelligence, Surveillance, and Reconnaissance" remains central to Fort Huachuca's mission, but in 2025 there were reports that the Museum was slated for closure.

127 **Inspired by interpretive signage** at the Millville Historic Townsite and Rock Art Discovery Trail, San Pedro Riparian National Conservation Area, AZ, 2021.

128 **Versioned from "The Wham Paymaster Robbery, 1889."** *Notorious and Noteworthy Cases of Crime and Punishment,* historical display at the Pima County Courthouse, Tucson, 2019. Gold and silver coins worth $28,000 were stolen (the poem gives this amount in its 2025 equivalent) and never recovered, becoming what's known as generational wealth.

129 **Inspired by "Cattle"** in Thomas E. Sheridan, *Arizona: A History,* rev. ed. (University of Arizona Press, 2012). Also Patricia Nelson Limerick, *The Legacy of Conquest: The Unbroken Past of the American West* (W. W. Norton, 1988).

131 **Inspired by the history** related in Lawrence Clayton, Jim Hoy, and Jerald Underwood, *Vaqueros, Cowboys, and Buckaroos* (University of Texas Press, 2001).

133 **Photograph** by author. "Buying More Caps for Kidme," 2025.

134 **Oil painting.** Marjorie Reed, "Tim & Judy's Tombstone," 1980.

136 **Photograph.** C. S. Fly, "Geronimo and Natches mounted, Natches with hat on; son of Geronimo standing by his side. This group photograph was taken by special request of Geronimo." From left to right are Perico, Geronimo, Naiche, and Tsisnah, 1886. See Jay Van Orden, "C. S. Fly at Cañon De Los Embudos: American Indians as Enemy in the Field—A Photographic First," *Journal of Arizona History* 30, no. 3 (Autumn 1989): 319–346.

137 **Photograph.** Tim Phillips, "Jefferson Davis Milton Exhibit," ca. 1983. While this particular exhibit no longer exists, another exhibit designed by Tim Phillips, "Tombstone's Founder: Ed Schieffelin," was still on display at Tombstone Courthouse State Park as of 2025.

138 **Photograph.** Bill Phillips, "Timmy and Uncle Lew," ca. 1955.

139 **Visual samples include:** Family photo. Elizabeth Mangelsdorf, "Air show visitors tour the giant C-5A Galaxy at Fort Huachuca," *The Arizona Daily Star,* October 26, 1987.

140 **Visual samples include:** Family photos. *The Tombstone Epitaph Local Edition,* April 22 to May 6, 1983. Frank J. Dobie, "Los Muertos No Hablan," *Coronado's Children* (Grosset & Dunlap, 1930).

141 **Visual samples include:** Family photos. Edward Dorn, "Mesoxoic Landscape," in *Way More West: New and Selected Poems* (Penguin Books, 2007), p. 135. "Map of the Tombstone mining district : Cochise Co., Arizona Ter.," San Francisco [Calif.]: Litho. H. S. Crocker, 1881, Library of Congress.

142 **Visual samples include:** Diagram of Stanislavski's System. Photograph of author as child. Bird Cage Theatre illustration from Martin, *Tombstone's Epitaph.* Perception System - Gestalt Principles.

143 **Photograph.** Tim Phillips, "Monsoon Seen from Woodhouse," ca. 1983.

144 **Photograph** by author. "Dragoons," ca. 1998. **Photograph.** Tim Phillips, "The '65 Ranchero," ca. 1983.

149 **Photograph.** Judy Phillips, "Tim and Logan at Tumacacori," 1983.

150 **". . . to help this desert survive us."** With gratitude to my colleague and friend Maegan Lopez for teaching me this framing of what we're here to do together.

154 **Photograph** by author. "From Sunset Rock, Dragoons," ca. 1994.

ACKNOWLEDGMENTS

This book has been many years in the making, and it only exists thanks to the many people who had a hand in it. My thanks to the staff of the University of Arizona Press: to Elizabeth Wilder, Leigh McDonald, Amanda Krause, and Kathryn Conrad, for taking on this unwieldy project, their patience, and their collaboration. Thank you, Mari Herreras, for being a true compañera at a moment when I needed it most.

I'm grateful to the University of Arizona MFA Creative Writing Program, which provided the time, space, and resources I needed to dig into this history. You all changed my life and creative practice for the better: Bojan Louis, Brandon Shimoda, Susan Briante, Ander Monson, Raquel Gutierrez, Farid Matuk, Manuel Muñoz, Alison Hawthorne Deming, Gabriel Dozal, Gabriel Palacios, Hea-Ream Lee, Lily Herman, Katerina Ivanov Prado, Jac Sipovic, Suyi Davies Okungbowa, Margo Steines, Natalie Lima, Aria Pahari, Kimberly Alidio, Matisse Rosen, and Marianna Ariel ColesCurtis. Thank you to Abigail Chabitnoy, Diana Arterian, and Justin St. Germain for their valuable feedback on earlier versions of this work. Lucy Kirkman, I'll miss you forever.

Adam Cooper-Terán, Nick Geogiou, Enrique García Naranjo, Meleena Karger, Sarita Gonzales, Amy Juan, Lydia Otero, Dolores Rivas Bahti, Gugulethu Moyo, Eva Sierra, Paola Valenzuela, Melani Martinez, Natasha Carrizosa, Jasminne Mendez, Gabriel Sullivan, Nat Brewster Nguyen: thank you for your art and for being accomplices in all the good things.

Thank you to Tyler Meier and the staff of the University of Arizona Poetry Center, and to Allison Miller, Jodie Chertudi, and Miguel Flores for manifesting so beautifully a mural version of poems from this book. Appreciation to the University of Arizona Libraries, Special Collections, which holds the only archive of *The Tombstone Eptitaph Local Edition* I've been able to track down (and which serendipitously includes *only* May 1982 through May 1983—ending with the issue with the birth announcement). Thank you, Frank Brown and (the old) Old Tucson Studios, for letting me wander a very decrepit Mescal movie set.

Infinite gratitude to Spring, Isadora, and Esme. Thank you for the many hours this book required and for helping to build a life that centers our artistic practices. Uncle Steve, DeeAnn, Jack, Cassidy, Dierks, Delanee, Bart, Shayne, Danica: Love y'all.

Mom, Dad, Ali: I love you with all of my deepest heart.
Thank you for this life and for teaching me how to love this complicated world.

ABOUT THE AUTHOR

Logan Phillips is a poet and cultural worker based in Tucson, Arizona (traditional lands of the Tohono O'odham). He is author of *Sonoran Strange*, alongside numerous poetry chapbooks and art books, including the NoVoGRAFíAS series (2010–present). A seasoned performer and collaborator, Phillips tours his work internationally, contributing to a wide range of arts, education, and land-based projects. Dirtyverbs.com.

For the audiobook, videos, tour dates, and more, please visit reckonbook.com.